COCKY GAMER

LAUREN HELMS

Cocky Gamer
Copyright © 2020 by Lauren Helms and Cocky Hero Club, Inc.
All rights reserved.
All rights reserved worldwide.

No part of this book may be reproduced, copied or transmitted in any medium, whether electronic, internet or otherwise, without the expressed permission of the author. This is a work of fiction. All characters, events, locations, and names occurring in this book are the product of the author's imagination or are the property of their respective owners and are used fictitiously. Any resemblances to actual events, locations, or persons (living or dead), is entirely coincidental and not intended by the author. All trademarks and trade names are used in a fictitious manner and are in no way endorsed by or an endorsement of their respective owners.

May contain sexual situations, violence, sensitive and offensive language, and mature topics.

Recommended for age 18 years and up.

Images © DepositPhotos – feedough
Cover Design © Aubree Valentine at Beyond the Bookshelf
Formatting: Beyond the Bookshelf
Editing: Amanda Cuff at Savage Hart Book Services
Proofreading: Yvette Deon

Contents

About Cocky Gamer and the Cocky Hero Club	vii
Playlist	xi
1. Ben	1
2. Kelly	8
3. Ben	17
4. Kelly	28
5. Ben	38
6. Kelly	52
7. Ben	65
8. Kelly	79
9. Ben	94
10. Kelly	103
11. Ben	117
12. Kelly	128
13. Ben	141
14. Kelly	152
15. Ben	163
16. Kelly	173
17. Kelly	180
18. Ben	191
19. Kelly	204
Epilogue	214
The Cocky Hero Club	221
Acknowledgments	223
Other Books by Lauren Helms	225
About the Author	227

About Cocky Gamer and the Cocky Hero Club

Cocky Gamer is a standalone story inspired by Vi Keeland and Penelope Ward's Cocky Bastard. It's published as part of the Cocky Hero Club world, a series of original works, written by various authors, and inspired by Keeland and Ward's *New York Times* bestselling series.

Would the real Garland Thorpe please stand up?

Playlist

Rescue Me - Isaac Butler
  Nice To Meet Ya - Niall Horan
  Lonely - Diplo, Jonas Brothers
  In Your Eyes (feat. Kenny G) Remix - The Weeknd, Kenny G
  Feel Alive - Katie Herzig
  Midnight (feat. Liam Payne) - Alesso, Liam Payne
  Somewhere Else - Delaney Jane
  One Day - Logan Smith
  the 1 - Taylor Swift
  Leap Of Faith - Christopher
  this is love - Walk Off the Earth
  I Found You - Andy Grammer

To listen to the full playlist, check it out on Spotify and on YouTube!

ONE

Ben

"I'm telling ya, man, we've got to hit up Club Punch while you're here." My buddy, Garland, chatters on about it next to me as we walk toward the little café he promised me has the best damn coffee in town.

"Meh," I reply and try not to bristle at his words. It's eight in the morning, and I've had a long night. The last thing I want to think about is a raging, loud, packed nightclub. Taking the last flight out of O'Hare last night landed me in LAX early this morning. With the time change, I didn't dare nap. Instead, I unpacked my stuff in my hotel room and tried like hell to stay awake. So, I'm going on more than a day without sleep. My last cup of joe was three hours ago after disembarking the plane. As long as I can get some liquid black-gold through my veins soon and continue to keep it pumping throughout the day, I should be fine for another ten hours or so.

Culver City, California, is a busy little city about twelve miles from Los Angeles. While I've only been here once before, it'll become a home away from home for the next year. I have a contract with Lasso, one of the top video game developers in the industry right now, to produce several voice-overs for three of their upcoming games. Being a professional video gamer has more perks than not, and if it hadn't been for being part of the top *Call of Battle* team last year, I wouldn't have gotten a chance to meet the head honcho at Lasso. Thanks to Garland, who also works at Lasso, I was able to get my name thrown into the ring for the highly sought-after voice of the main character in their next big game.

Tournament season for *Call of Battle* is gearing up, so I'll have to split my time between Chicago, my hometown and home base for Team NoMad, and Culver City over the next few months. I try to ignore the fact that my interest in my job is waning, but it's becoming more and more the norm. Normally, I'd hunker down and spend all my hours playing *CoB*, and studying the game to come up with new strategies. But for some reason, I welcome the change in scenery.

I thought my teammates would be annoyed to learn I was going to be taking on this side gig, but they were surprisingly supportive. That kind of makes them sound like assholes, but they really aren't. While I'm not super close to the team of four other pro gamers, I do consider them friends. Dex, Simon, Bernie, and Chuck have been my teammates for several years now. While I'm closest to Chuck, I haven't known him as long as the others. Bernie has become a closer friend than I expected, but she's just so damn friendly, it's hard not to like her. Dex and Simon are cool, but I don't spend a lot of my free time with them. I've got other friends and a life outside of professional gaming, which is why I think it's time for me to start thinking about what comes after my time with the team.

I might not come across as a very social dude, but I pay attention to what's going on around me, and Team NoMad is changing. It's been at a snail's pace, but it's changing. And I'm not going to sit around with my thumbs up my ass when I find out there's no more team. I make a shit-ton of money being as good as I am at *CoB*, and being on a championship winning team several years in a row only makes the reward sweeter. But I can't live off sponsorships for the rest of my days. Not that those will last much longer after I retire from the professional gaming world. And unlike the only retired Team NoMad member, Link, I'm not interested in building a YouTube empire. I'm more of a behind-the-scenes kind of guy, so voice-overs for the video games themselves—hell yeah, sign me up. At least this side gig will provide me some time to figure out exactly what I want to do. Maybe it will even help me slide right into the next chapter of my kick-ass life. Let's be honest, what kid doesn't want to get paid to play video games all day? I'm already living my best life, but it's just about time for a new dream, I guess.

The chime of the bell above the door announces our arrival, but I suspect it goes unnoticed due to the sound of grinding coffee beans and whirling blenders overtop the murmur of voices and laughter. The baristas behind the counter are all busy filling the orders of the customers that form a rather impressive line down the side of the shop. Freshly brewed coffee with a hint of caramel and spices tingle my nose as I inhale. There's always something to be said about a coffee shop and its immediate effect that it has on your senses. It's the first time I've ever stepped foot inside the Melting Moon Café, yet I can tell it won't be the last. I need coffee like I need air, so this place will become my refuge.

Long twinkle lights hang from the ceiling mimicking stars, and there's a full-wall mural of a night sky complete with a large moon covering the wall near the entrance.

There's a mix of bistro tables with trendy wrought iron chairs and padded seats, and overstuffed leather chairs are spaced out in the comfortable lobby. A wooden staircase at the far end of the café leads to a second-floor landing that covers half the space. From what I can see, large tables are spread out overlooking the busy streets of Culver City thanks to floor to ceiling windows.

"I love the smell of coffee in the morning," Garland moans next to me.

"Morning, noon, or night; the time doesn't matter to me," I reply, taking in a deep, satisfying breath.

"Only a night owl like yourself can handle coffee at any hour of the day. My last cup can't come after one p.m. or I'm up all night. And you know how much I love my sleep." He shakes his head.

I chuckle and thump his shoulder. "Do you still have to sleep with a sound machine next to your pillow like you did when we were kids?"

Glaring at me, he replies, "No, I've upgraded to an app. It's number one in the app store for health and wellness, so clearly I'm not the only one who needs a little help chasing the ZZZs at night."

Garland Thorpe has been one of my closest friends since we were nine, and even though we live on nearly opposite sides of the country, we remain good friends. We both shared the dream of working in the video game industry. His journey took him to California where a good number of video game developers headquarter to make video game magic, whereas I didn't have to go far when a pro gaming team more or less knocked on my door. Five years later, he's working for Lasso as a project manager.

The line is long, but it's moving quickly. Tension falls from my shoulders as I realize I'll soon have coffee flowing through my system. As a night owl, morning isn't my favorite.

We move closer to the promised land where a long counter covered in dark wood tiles is stacked with chrome espresso and frothing machines. A glass case to the left of the registers showcases a selection of snacks such as muffins, cookies, and pastries. My stomach grumbles as I spy what looks to be a giant chocolate muffin with chocolate chips.

As we move forward again, I skim the chalkboard wall behind the counter where it lists the menu. Just as I get to the list of mochas and lattes, my focus is pulled toward a couple standing near the registers. The woman stands facing a man with her hand on her hip. Anguish and frustration pour out of her, and I get antsy hoping she doesn't make a scene. I'm not in the mood to witness a lovers' quarrel this morning.

The poor sod doesn't know what hits him as her voice climbs, causing more and more heads to turn toward them. Beside me, Garland elbows me and nods toward the couple, a sly grin on his face. A public shaming must be right up his alley this morning.

"Did you just check her out?" the woman seethes. He replies quietly, but her eyes go wide at his words. "I can't believe you, Dean. I'm standing right here!" the woman strikes.

The dude looks around as he mutters something to her again, clearly not wanting to make a scene.

Too late, brother.

"They all warned me you had a wandering eye, but no, I didn't listen. You're such an asshole!" Her voice hits a note that has me hoping management steps in soon. The dull ache that's been forming behind my tired eyes starts to throb, but my gaze is glued to the show just like the rest of the customers.

"Ah, snap! Dude better protect himself. She looks like she's squaring up to send that knee flying," Garland says with amusement. I nod, silently cursing myself for not being able to look away. The poor guy is about to lose his manhood in the middle of this busy café, and if someone handed me a bucket of popcorn, I'd take it willingly.

Just then, as if a director called for more comic relief, in near slow motion, a young woman stumbles right in front of the fighting couple. Her coffee goes flying toward both the screamer and her soon-to-be ex. Then, the girl stubs her foot on a nearby chair and launches face-first into the dude. Damn, this chick is clumsy. The guy has quick reflexes, and he reaches out and catches the poor girl from a nasty and embarrassing face-plant into the nearby table. A collective gasp rattles the café as he steadies her.

The angry girlfriend now wears Miss Clumsy's coffee with her horrifying expression.

Damn, why can't I look away from this train wreck?

Clumsy's wavy brown hair falls in her face as she feverishly apologizes to the couple. She's shaking as she moves her locks out of the way. Her cheeks are fire engine red with embarrassment. I instantly feel bad for her as I realize how damn cute she is. Not that I wouldn't feel bad for her if she wasn't cute, of course. But just as I notice, so does the dude who's doomed. He switches off his confused expression, and it turns into a sly, up-to-no-good smile.

Ah, shit.

Garland makes a nose next to me as he's thinking the same thing.

"Are you fucking kidding me, Dean? Did you just grab her ass? Right in front of me?" she shrills, and the poor girl winces, shoving the dude's grabby hands away from her.

"I'm so, so sorry," she pleads with the banshee, but her words go unnoticed. Thankfully for her, the man with the wandering hands is no longer paying her any attention as he defends himself. I barely hear his lame excuse for his behavior as I watch the cute, clumsy girl sneak around them, pick up her now empty cup of coffee, and slink away from the scene. As Garland and I move up to the counter, I turn and watch over my shoulder as she slinks out the door.

Garland laughs next to me, and I pull my gaze back to the couple just as a barista tells them to move their argument outside before mopping up the rest of the rogue coffee.

When we finally get to the front, Garland orders an Americano and nudges me to place my order, effectively bringing the morning soap opera to an end with no *to be continued* for the crowd.

"Nah, I got it, man," I tell him.

"Nope, while you're here on business, I've got you. All the coffee and drama," he waves to the couple still yelling at each other as they head to the doors, "you want. It's all on Lasso, my friend."

A guy could get used to unlimited free coffee, so I grin and order a large black coffee and a muffin.

Moments later, as we leave Melting Moon Café, I wonder about the cute, clumsy girl and how her day could possibly turn out after a morning like she had. I wonder how her side of the story will compare to all the other "you won't believe what I witnessed this morning…" stories that are sure to circulate throughout the day.

TWO

Kelly

At a near run, I dodge tables, chairs, and onlookers as I race for the exit. It's as if someone purposely placed several hurdles in the only path of my escape, and I'm surprised I don't fall over again. When I reach the double doors, I try to yank one open and find it doesn't budge. *Shit.* Seeing the large white decal that says *PUSH* right in front of my face, I push the door open and the cool breeze of freedom surrounds me.

I join the throes of pedestrians all hustling to their destination. It isn't until I take my second deep breath that I realize it's drizzling out. I slow to a leisurely pace, sure that I'm free from any lingering gazes, and dig around in my messenger bag for my umbrella. Short of dumping out the entire contents of my laptop case, I rifle through until I realize I left it at home. I close my eyes as my face slacks in disappointment. It doesn't rain much in Southern California, maybe less than forty days a year, so when you see rain on the forecast, you prepare.

Unless you're me, Kelly Spenser, showing up unprepared and with the worst possible timing. *Jeez Louise, this day is off to an amazing start.* I'm only about three blocks from the offices of Hill House Accounting, the CPA firm where I'm an admin assistant. So as long as the rain doesn't pick up, I can throw my hair up and try to touch up my makeup. Maybe I can fix myself before anyone else gets into the office. The last thing I need is to look like a drowned cat. I peek at my watch and sigh in relief as I note I'll be a good forty minutes early if I hurry now.

I really don't like spending more time than I have to in the office. But since my morning routine of cozying up in an over-stuffed chair while getting in some morning reading was interrupted by a couple clearly in need of counseling, I'll have to deal. What I don't love having to deal with is missing out on the best coffee in town and having to suck it up and drink the nasty stuff brewed in the lobby at work. I come to a stop with the crowd as we wait for the traffic light to signal it's safe to cross. Hunkering into my new pink jacket, I brace myself against the chilly water spitting from the gray sky. Just as the hoard of people start to move, my eyes bulge and a scream rips from my mouth as a spray of ice-cold, smelly water splashes across my body. A car screeches to a halt in the street next to me, treating me and a few others to a dirty street puddle shower. Those around me yell and curse the driver, who just honks and waves away the disgruntled pedestrians.

I look down to see my new coat is no longer a pretty shade of pink, my gray pant leg clings to me, and I'm now soaked to the bone. My bottom lip trembling, I clutch my fists together and will my anxiety to calm down.

Breathe, Kelly, breathe.

I move forward with the lingering walkers as the crosswalk signal starts its ten-second countdown. The rest of the walk to work is thankfully uneventful. Once I arrive, I've got about twenty minutes until the rest of my team starts trickling in to start this horrid Tuesday. Hill House Accounting is a large firm that employs a little under forty mostly uptight accountants, auditors, and other finance types. My particular team handles the company's personal finances such as payroll, outbound and inbound billing, and other general accounting. While I don't have a background in finance, my business degree gives me the knowledge to handle just about any admin assistant position in any professional office. It also means I'm normally the low man on the totem pole and deal with bosses and coworkers who aren't shy about sharing their specialties. I will concede that my boss and CFO of the company, Mr. Bales, never looks down on my lack of specialty, but he also doesn't seem to think I have potential for growth within the company. To be honest, I don't want to climb the finance ladder anyway. At least he's not as bad as my last boss, Amy Lin, at my short-lived receptionist position with an estate planning lawyer. She ran a tight ship as the assistant to both the attorneys who owned the firm. She did things old school and didn't have a problem with me knowing she was having an affair with one of the married partners. They fought a lot, and I only lasted two months before I couldn't take it anymore. Office drama is not my cup of tea.

I don't know why I continue to find myself in so many awkward situations, especially in the office. Heck, I can track it back to when I was working at my first law firm, Sherman, Kline, & Lefave, LLP, when my friend, Aubrey Bateman would use me as a buffer to her awkward as hell meetings with her now husband, Chance. I'm embarrassed to admit I let it happen more than once.

I sigh to myself as I detour to the fifth-floor women's restroom. Someday I'll find a job I love. I have to figure out what the hell I want to do with my life first, though.

I drop my bag onto the counter with a plop and assess the situation standing in front of me in the mirror.

Well, shit. I look like a drowned cat.

I start by taking my near ruined jacket off and gingerly laying it next to my bag. Then, I grab a handful of paper towels and blot my face down before trying to soak up any access water from my pant leg. I should probably just go home and shoot Mr. Bales an email telling him I'm taking a sick day. I could probably sneak out of here unnoticed.

I'm nearly settled on my decision when a stall door opens, and out pops Mr. Bales's right-hand woman, Laura Shaw. She's not my biggest fan, and that's fine with me. I've secretly been pouring orange juice in her office plants every time she requests watering them as one of my tasks as an assistant. The woman is in her forties, unmarried, works about eighty hours a week, and loves flaunting her controller-ship around the office. You couldn't pay me to even *wish* I had her job, but she's convinced we all want to be her. *No, thank you.*

With her nose stuck in the air, she sneers at me in the mirror. "Wow, Kelly, you look like something my poodle dragged in."

I dig around in my bag for my face wipes and try not to make direct eye contact with her. "I forgot my umbrella and had an unfortunate run-in with a mud puddle in the street." I wipe my face down, removing all traces of mud and raccoon eyes.

She chuckles as she finishes washing her hands. "Sounds like another example of why you'll never make it in corporate America, Kelly. Don't walk to work without an umbrella when it's raining." She shakes her head as she turns off the faucet. "Well, I'll be sure to let Mr. Bales know not to expect you on your A game today. We have an important conference call, so I'll request another assistant to step in to make sure you don't drop the ball anymore today."

I bite my tongue and force myself not to roll my eyes at the nasty witch. She leaves the restroom just as I find I've also left my emergency makeup kit at home. This is what I get for switching bags five minutes before it was time to leave for work. I stare myself down in the mirror and see stringy damp hair and a pale, makeup-less face that has seen more bad luck than anyone should in the forty minutes since they left their apartment.

I look utterly miserable.

I fight back tears of frustration as I hear my phone ring from inside my bag. Briefly, I weigh the chances of this call being just another tick in the bad day column and ignoring it. Who could possibly need me this early in the day? Did I break a mirror I'm not aware of? Did I cross the path of a black cat or walk under a ladder? I don't know what's brought on this current bout of bad luck, but I throw caution to the wind and decide to see who's calling.

Relief rushes through me when I see Aubrey's face fill my screen, and I slide my thumb over the screen to answer.

"Hey, Aubs," I sigh into the phone.

"Kell, you all right?" Her tone is laced with concern.

"Uh, it's been a day," I tell her, collecting my stuff and heading to my cubical. My run-in with Laura ruined my plan to call in sick. She'd know it was just to save face.

"It's not even nine yet. How can you be having a day?" she teases.

"Well, it started with no hot water this morning. Then I left my umbrella at home, ended up in the middle of a lovers' quarrel, and just got splashed with cold, muddy street water as I was waiting to cross the street." I let out a shaky breath.

"Shit. You are having a day," she says with pity.

"I'm glad you called, though. You always put a smile on my face," I tell her. And it's the truth. I've known Aubrey for a couple of years now, and she's grown into one of my closest friends. We weren't immediate friends, and it wasn't until she left the firm that our friendship grew. She and I stayed in touch via social media, which led to visits and dinners when I'd visit her home city, Hermosa Beach. Now, we talk nearly every day and see each other most weekends, if only to get coffee. Speaking of which, I may need to find a new coffee spot to frequent since the whole place watched that hot mess of a breakup scene I stumbled into.

"You know I have a sixth sense about those closest to me. I always know when Chance is up to no good, and I always seem to know when you need a friend." It's all true. Chance is almost always up to no good, and she does have a habit of knowing when I need a GIF or funny video to brighten my day. "But let's go back to that lovers' quarrel for a second. Explain."

"Oh my God, Aubs. It was horrible. It's been a while since I've utterly embarrassed myself in public. Maybe since my junior year of college when I took a nasty tumble down the forum's stairs in front of a hundred and fifty students, ending up with a nasty bruise on my ass and a sprained ankle." I ponder for a moment, stuck in my memory.

"Ah, all right. And this morning?" she urges me to continue.

"Right, well, I tripped. And I don't know what I tripped *on* exactly, but I fell into the middle of a couple fighting. Once I realized my coffee was all over them and the floor, a chair, like, came out of nowhere, and my foot got tangled in it. I literally fell into the dude getting belittled by his girlfriend. He caught me from face-planting into the table, but he didn't keep his hands to himself. So, *of course*, that launched the girlfriend into a crazy tangent. I snuck out of there without further complications, but it was not my finest moment."

Laughter erupts from the other end of the line as I give Aubrey a moment. I'm not mad; I'd laugh, too, if the roles were reversed.

"Shit. My gosh, Kelly, that's crazy." She tries—and fails—to catch her breath amidst the laughter.

"Yup."

"Was the place packed? Like, how big of a scene are we talking?" she asks.

"I was in Melting Moon, so you know it was packed. And the whole place was watching the fallout while I made my ungraceful entrance."

She gasps and says, "Oh, God!" through another round of laughter.

"Honestly," I add, "I'd put money on it that someone got it on camera."

"Chance, come here," she yells, all too quick to share my embarrassment. "Get your phone and pull up Twitter."

"You called, Princess?" I hear Chance ask. I bite back a groan, knowing he's going to hear about my morning and will *never* let me live it down. Aubrey tells him to pull up the social media app and search for Melting Moon Café, and sure enough, I hear the couple from the café fighting.

"Oh, snap. Someone got the whole fight and posted it. It's trending," Aubrey's shocked voice declares over the video they're watching on Chance's phone.

"Is that Kelly?" Chance asks, and then they both start laughing.

"Kelly, I'm so sorry for laughing, but it's just such an amazing video." She's wheezes, trying to calm herself, and I smile as I wait for my computer to boot up.

"Honestly, it's the most action I've seen in months," I tell her honestly. "Once I get over my initial shock, I'll mark it down as a successful day."

"Oh, stop it. Though, he did get a good grab of your ass. I would have smacked him," she replies, and I hear Chance in the background rattling on about how he would have punched a brother out for the grab if it had been her.

"Yeah, well, I was in shock," I gripe.

"Are you coming out to see me this weekend?" she asks, and I'm thankful for the subject change. "You gonna catch some waves while you're here?"

"I was planning on it. Will you be around?" She and Chance are always around, but I still ask.

"Yup. And while you're here, I want to make you dinner. I've got a job opportunity for you. Also, I want to set you up on a date."

I clench my jaw. "Aubs," I whine, "no dates! But I'll take you up on the dinner. And, of course, I'm curious about this opportunity." I don't add that I won't hold my breath. My luck with jobs is about the same as my luck with dates. Bad—as experience shows.

"Oh, don't whine. I'll see you this weekend. Text me later, and I promise I won't let Chance retweet that video anymore," she rushes.

I gasp. "He's sharing it?"

"K, bye." She kisses into the phone and the line goes dead.

Dropping my head into my hands, I sigh. Co-workers have started filling in around the office, and I note that my workday has officially started. I throw myself into my work and start marking things off my task list. But before long, my mind travels back to the café this morning and that stupid tweet with proof of my unfortunate fall. I stuff my earbuds into my pocket and walk to the other end of the floor, ducking into the restroom furthest away from my department's offices. I pull up Twitter and see that Chance just tweeted out a picture of his goat, Pixy, standing in a big flower bed. I click his name and find the previous tweet, his retweet of the incident at Melting Moon Café. Shoving my buds into my ears, I watch my Internet debut.

Fuck my life.

It's been retweeted more than a thousand times.

THREE

Ben
___

I've been in my fair share of nightclubs over the years. Dex and the rest of the team enjoy a night out after a big win. But the strobe lights pulsing inside the room, having to scream into your friend's ear for them to hear you, and the smell of sweat mixed with hundreds of different perfumes and colognes is a setup for disappointment. I prefer to get wasted and stupid in the confines of my own place or hotel room. Yet sometimes, to avoid being referred to as unsocial, I tag along. However, when Garland told me I had to come out to Club Punch with him tonight, I didn't want to turn him down.

I've been jonesing for something new—something different. And I've decided to start this new shit of saying yes when I would normally say no. Garland and a few guys from Lasso come here often when they have a guest DJ or live music, and I'll admit, this place is pretty sweet. Small round high-tops line the perimeter of the room, and there's a large dance floor in front of a stage and DJ booth. There are hundreds of people here tonight, but the club is so large, there's still plenty of room as groups of people hang out together.

"Dude, I told you this place was sick." Garland leans toward me from across the table, yelling to ensure I hear him.

I nod while I continue to take in the scene. There is a second story—for VIPs, I assume—but my gaze is drawn to the flow of the place. Well-muscled bouncers check IDs at the front while two scantily clad women stamp hands at a table nearby.

"I know it's not your normal scene," Garland yells, "but it doesn't get crazy. And the music and drinks are stellar. Their house DJ is fire, and I'd be surprised if they keep him much longer before he cuts an album and makes it big time in the industry."

"No, man, it's pretty tight. I'd come back." I raise my voice and lift my beer only to find it's empty. "I'm going to head to the bar. Do you want another?" I ask, tipping my head to his drink.

He nods. "Yeah, and get their house sampler. I need to get some carbs in my belly if I'm going to keep drinking."

I chuckle as I push out of my chair. "It's a Thursday night, Gar. You going to get wasted?"

"Not if I don't carb load as I drink." He grins.

Shaking my head at his antics, I head to the long bar at the back of the room. I push past people mingling, trying not to press against them as it seems a new surge of folks have arrived. So much for this place not getting overcrowded. Finally making it to the bar, I find a spot where two seats sit open.

I make eye contact with one of the three bartenders behind the bar, and she shimmies toward me. I order another beer on tap and a Jack and Coke for Garland. She sets down our drinks while she puts in my food order. I'm surprised they even have food on the menu, but this place just moved up another notch in my mind.

The temperature is cool, but the linger of stale beer and pot wafts through the air. I take a long swig of my beer and the cold drink slides down my throat. I resist the urge to sigh when I pull the glass away. Damn, that's good beer. Just as I set down my glass, a body rams into me from the side. Jerking forward, I grip my beer, and relief that I didn't lose it floods my veins. But then I remember why I'm relieved and look over my shoulder as I see a smallish figure looking down at her shoes. Turning toward her, I realize she's only a few inches shorter than me, and she's saying something I can't quite hear over the music.

"Are you okay?" I yell.

She doesn't look up at me, her gaze glued to the ground. "Yeah, I just don't understand," she says. Her words are louder now, but her voice is muffled. She seems confused, and I start to dread I might be dealing with a drunk girl. I peek at my watch and see it's only nine. If she's already wasted, then she either started early or she's a lightweight. I tentatively reach out and graze the side of her arm to garner her attention. Her warm flesh prickles at my touch, and I bite back a knowing grin. Her thick, wavy hair moves to the side as she looks up at me. Big, round eyes fill my view, and I take a step back, right into the lip of the bar. I recognize this girl, but from where, I have no fucking clue.

"I am so sorry for bumping into you," she shouts. She's still focused on the ground in front of her.

I mentally shake out my confusion as I drop my hand from her elbow. "I'd say it was a little more than a bump. More like a fall or a plunge."

Her eyes appraise me to figure out if I'm being a douche—which I am—but only because I'm shit at flirting.

So, I grin and give it another try. "All I mean is, you came at me pretty hard, so I hope you're all right. Did you lose something?"

She narrows her eyes. "Is this is an attempt at a shitty pick-up line?"

I chuckle. "No. Did you lose something?" I point to the ground. "You were looking for something."

Her face slacks. "Oh, no." She looks down again, twisting her body around. "I was looking for whatever I tripped on."

"Did you find it?" I ask, looking around as well. I don't see a single culprit.

"No, but with my track record lately, I could trip on air if the moment was right. Or wrong," she mumbles.

It's hard to hear her when she isn't looking at me. I have the sudden urge to gain the attention of those dark eyes again, so I reach out and touch her arm—again. She stops looking around, and I've accomplished my goal. Even though she's a complete stranger, I feel this pull between us. There's a sense of familiarity that drives me to want to know more about her.

"Do you need to get a drink?" As I gesture to the bar at my back, she nods, smiles, and steps up next to me. She faces the bar just as a plate of fried food is placed in front of me.

"Can I get another drink?" I ask the bartender and I look to the woman next to me. She asks for a Long Island Iced Tea, and while she settles onto the stool next to me, I take a moment to take her in. A lot of the ladies here tonight are dressed to the nines in skintight, cleavage-revealing tops and dresses. But this woman is wearing a dark tank top that shows off just enough and well-fitting, cut-off jean shorts. My eyes travel down her long, toned legs to find a pair of black and white Converse slip-ons.

She looks comfortable and puts off a low-key, low-maintenance vibe. I fucking dig it.

"So you tripped. Do you do that often?" I ask, leaning one elbow into the bar, fully facing her. She looks down longingly at the plate of tots, chicken fingers, onion rings, and mozzarella sticks. *Huh, that does look good.* I didn't even know what I was ordering, but now I can see why Garland wanted it. He'll have to wait for his food and drink, though. I'm a bit preoccupied at the moment.

Looking up at me, she studies my face. I'm sure she's trying to figure out the intent of my question. I'm just trying to flirt with her, so I give her a small smile.

She smiles back and nods. "Meh, I have my moments. This week has not been good to me." She eyes my plate again, and I can almost see the drool fall from her mouth.

As I nudge the pile of fried goodness toward her, her eyes go wide. "Help yourself. I'm starving, but I doubt I can eat this all on my own." Sure, I ordered this for Garland. But since he's not standing here right now and I paid for it, I'll gladly share with the lady who appreciates good food.

She doesn't hesitate—which I appreciate—and grabs a tot and pops it into her mouth. Her face contorts, and I hear a faint moan of pleasure as the rich flavor hits her tongue. Damn.

"Good, huh?" I ask and snag up a tot for myself before dunking it in the dish of ketchup.

"Yeah. I didn't have dinner, so I'm sorry if I'm going to town on ya." She gulps down another tot, and while the room is pretty dark, I see her eyes close as she replays what she said in her head. I chuckle and shake my head. She's fun.

"Well, I'm totally cool with you going to town." I wink, and she covers her mouth with her hand and giggles. I'd really like to get to know her more, so I keep the conversation flowing. "What brings you out to Club Punch tonight?"

"Oh, my cousin's birthday party. She loves this place. You?" She takes a sip of her drink, and I can't help but watch the way her lips cover the straw.

"Nice. Happy birthday to your cousin. This is my first time here. A buddy of mine talked me into coming out tonight." I leave out the fact I'm from out of town.

"This place is pretty bumping. Clubs aren't really my scene, but if I have to go out, this is where I go." She turns slightly toward me and takes in the club while she talks.

I don't know if it's being in the crowded club, or if her proximity is just too much to handle, but it's getting hot in here. The sleeves on my button-down are rolled halfway up my forearm, but I push them up toward my elbow. The movement catches her eye, and she stares at my arms for longer than she should. I smirk, knowing the ink up and down my arms has her attention.

My personality and looks paired with my profession is an odd combo, I know. Being a pro gamer, you'd automatically assume I'm a nerd. And maybe I am, but I dropped the pocket protector years ago. The ink on my body helps me come across as a bigger badass than I am. I'm more of a lover than a fighter—unless I'm dealing with some newb on Call of Battle who can't keep his fucking mouth shut about how good he isn't. Then all bets are off.

The ladies are normally perplexed by my look when they find out my profession. I've witnessed the confusion on their faces before. Just a few months ago, one woman flat out told me she didn't believe I was a gamer, that I looked like I belonged to a motorcycle club. I chuckled at that. Sometimes it works for me and sometimes it doesn't.

I take a swig of my beer. "You like ink?" I ask.

She snaps out of her stare and clears her throat. "I'm actively choosing to not be embarrassed for how long I stared."

"No need to be. I like that you're curious."

That earns me a smile. "I just wasn't expecting to see tattoos. And, yeah, I guess I like them."

Her eyes flit down to my forearm where the end of a gaming joystick peeks out from my shirt. It's one of my favorite pieces. It took several sessions, as it covers most of my arm and features five popular game controllers. It's epic. It's the only gamer related tat I have, so it's special.

"Do you have any tats?" I eye her, trying to figure out where a girl like her would hide ink.

"I do," tilting her head, she smirks. "You're trying to figure out where, aren't you?" She snorts.

I snap my eyes to her face and see the playfulness there, her smile is sexy as sin. "You caught me." She shakes her head and laughs before taking another drink.

Placing my elbow on the bar, I lean my chin onto my hand and ask, "How many, and where are they?" I tilt toward her with raised eyebrows.

"Hmm. Wouldn't you like to know?" She winks, then snags a mozzarella stick and dunks it in the marinara. Shamelessly, I watch her tongue dart out and lick the end of the stick to catch the drip of sauce.

Fuck. Me.

Clearing my throat, I direct our conversation toward safer topics such as the club and her cousin. We chat some more as a couple more songs fade into the next. Then, I'm bumped into again.

What the hell?

"Shit," I mutter as Garland thumps me on the back. "Did you trip?" I growl.

He looks down and then back up at us. "Kind of? It

was slippery, but I don't see anything." Next to me comes a giggle.

We both look at my companion. "Same thing happened to me," she tells Garland. He takes her in, eyes her from head to toe, and within seconds, I'm fighting off the urge to stake my claim. I'm not normally the jealous type, and Garland and I've never fought over the opposite sex before, but I guess there's always a first time for everything.

"Hello, pretty lady." He grins. She smiles back, but she's giving him that same appraising look she gave me when she thought I was hitting on her.

"Seems as if you've made a new friend, Benny Boy. What's this beautiful creature's name?" He chuckles, not taking his eyes off her. I've always known Garland to handle himself with confidence and finesse, so I'm puzzled as to why he's acting like such a fool right now.

"Shut up, Garland," I sneer at the use of his annoying as fuck nickname.

"I'm Kelly, thanks for asking. Benny Boy, over here, hasn't even asked my name yet." She smiles and shoots me a challenging grin. Well, damn, she's right.

"He didn't get the nickname Benny Boy for no reason." Garland laughs, and I flex my fist at my side.

"I've never been called by that name, so cut it out." I look at Kelly then. "It's just Ben, by the way. If anyone wants to talk names, let's talk about Garland," I joke, knowing it's a sore subject for him.

His eyes narrow slightly at me, but his chin juts out as he tries to remain casual. "It's a family name."

"Well, I dig it," Kelly says, giving him her support. I roll my eyes. Damn it, Garland. Of course, he'd win sympathy from the chick I'm totally digging on right now.

Garland moves closer, crowding the space between us

and effectively severing my closeness with Kelly. He eyes me with a raised eyebrow and a look that screams, *See?* I smash my lips together and give him a warning look, and he chuckles in return.

"What do you need, Garland?" I spit out.

"I came to see what was taking you so long to bring back our drinks and my—oh, look, my dinner," he says when he looks down at the half-empty plate of food. Payback's a bitch, and I just shrug.

"Oh my gosh. I'm so sorry for eating your food," Kelly blurts out.

I cut into their little conversation. "Don't make her feel bad, Gar. I told her she could have some. Then I started eating too, and the time got away from me. Look, here's your drink. It's still cold and everything." I grab his drink and maneuver it in front of him.

"Thanks," he grumbles. He eyeballs me, and I give him the universal look for, *Beat it, buddy*. And he finally gets it. "No apologies needed, darling Kelly. My food is your food."

I scowl at his comment, but he continues to address Kelly and doesn't even notice my glare. "I'm gonna head back to my table. I'll leave you two here to get to know each other." Garland bows his head toward her, and he slowly backs away and then disappears into the crowd.

Holding my breath, I look at Kelly. As soon as we make eye contact, she bursts out in laughter.

"Wow, that was…" she trails off, her humor taking over.

"I know, he's something else. And by the way, I paid for that drink and the food, so don't let him make you think it was actually his." I offer her a bemused smile.

She smiles back, and I can't look away from her mesmerizing eyes. I wonder what color they are; it's too dark in here to tell. Heat pools in her cheeks as she bites her lip, and I want to suck that lip into my mouth.

She leans in slightly and I follow suit.

I'm going to kiss her. *Fuck yeah!* I'm going to kiss this gorgeous woman whom I just met at the bar of some hip club. I'm going to kiss her, then I'm going to see if I can get her to come back to my hotel room with me. I close the gap between us, our lips just a whisper apart when a whoosh of cool air hits my face. I blink and see that Kelly still sits next to me, but her focus is on the two women standing next to her.

"Ohmigod! Kelly, we've been looking for you," they squeal, their words jumbled together. I swallow hard, lean back, and try to play it cool. But fuck that shit.

"I told you I was going to the bar," Kelly answers, and she nervously looks back at me. I can see the remorse in her eyes, but I smile and hope I come across as cool as a fucking cucumber. That's when they notice me. The taller of the two giggles and waves at me as she elbows the shorter woman. I don't get any flirty reception from this one. No, I'm greeted with a glare as she grabs ahold of Kelly's hand.

"Kelly, I need to talk to you." She starts to pull Kelly away from me, and it takes everything in me not to grab her other hand and pull her toward me.

Kelly looks over her shoulder at me and yells as she's yanked away. "I'm so sorry, Ben. I'll be back." She flashes me a small smile, and I tip my head in acknowledgment.

Fuck.

She walks away and the crowd eats her up. I was about to seal the deal with a sexy as fuck stranger on my last night in Culver City, but now I suspect I won't see her again.. Our chemistry was through the roof hot, and I was looking forward to finding those hidden tattoos. I drop my head in disappointment when I realize I never got her number. So, like the desperate son of a bitch I am, I wait for her.

After what seems like hours, I realize she's not coming back. I close out my tab and text Garland that I'm leaving. I don't bother to correct him when he asks if I'm leaving with the sexy lady from the bar. I head back to my hotel, silently cursing the club, Garland, and the grumpy friend who pulled Kelly away before what I suspect would have been a hot fucking kiss.

FOUR

Kelly

"I wouldn't be surprised if cobwebs are growing in your vajayjay." Darcy giggles from the couch as I slip on my heels. I sneer and then huff when I wobble as I stand on one foot.

"Come on, you know it's a possibility," she pushes. "It's been, what, a year since you've hooked up with a dick?"

"You say that as if I've hooked up with a vagina in the meantime," I say, regaining my balance now that I'm back on two feet.

"Well, I'm not going to judge if that's the case, Kell."

I glance at her, and while her expression is light, I can tell she's being serious. "Oh, stop. I always have been, and always will be, into the D. And it hasn't been a year. Maybe only, like, six or seven months." I roll my eyes again and look for my purse.

She leans to her side, reaching for something. "Maybe this date with Sam will quench your dry spell." She snorts, handing me my purse, which was sitting on the end table.

"This is a blind date, Darcy. I don't even know the guy. What makes you think a first date will turn into a hookup?" I peek at my phone and see I've got to get going. I hate being late, but I almost always am.

"You were going to go home with that dude from Punch a few weeks ago," Darcy challenges, and I find myself annoyed she brought him up. She totally clam jammed me, and I'm still shitty about it.

"First of all, his name is Ben, and I was getting to know him. There was something between us and you ruined it." I glare at her as I head for the door.

"Pfft. You should be thanking me! He wasn't your type. He was tall, dark, and broody. Way too many tats, so he was probably a bad boy. Not your type." She waves her hand as if to brush off my concern. "And if you were planning on hooking up with a stranger, what's keeping you from hooking up with Sam tonight?" she challenges. I stop momentarily, my hand on the doorknob. She's got a point.

Gathering my thoughts, I look at her over my shoulder. "I'm not a one-night stand kinda girl, Darcy. You know this. But I met a guy who I clicked with, and I would have been that kind of girl for a night with him." Guilt flicks across her face as I continue. "The chances of me meeting another guy I feel that with right off the bat are unlikely. Not with the luck I've been having lately. But I promise you, if I feel anything for Sam, I won't brush it aside. I'll pursue him if he's feeling it, too."

She accepts my promise and tells me to have a good night as I leave the apartment.

As I grab an Uber, I can't shake my thoughts on Ben. She's right—he's not my normal type. I go for the clean-cut good guys, and Ben is the opposite of that. He has thick, perfectly messy dark hair, and dark brows and eyes. His smile hit me right in the lady bits every time he flashed those white teeth of his. When he rolled up his sleeves, I saw that dark ink covered his arms, and I couldn't stop staring. I wanted to explore the art and find out why he had it marked forever on his skin.

Like I said, I'm not a one-night stand kind of girl. I like relationships. Relationships are steady, predictable, safe. It's been nearly two years since I've been in one, and I'm not ashamed to admit that I miss it. I've causally, but exclusively dated over the past two years, but that's the extent of it. And the men either wanted more or less exclusivity. I didn't feel a spark worth turning into more with either of them. Six or seven months later—I'm trying not to keep track—I'm officially in a dry spell.

The car rolls near the casual restaurant I'm meeting Sam at. Heading inside, I grab a small table when I realize I'm early. *Wow, that never happens.* I mentally fist pump myself.

I take in Luigi's Italiano—it's one of my favorite little Italian eateries. Their pasta is handmade in the shop, and their sauces are delectably rich and flavorful. Several tables are occupied, and the sound of the patrons' soft murmurs and laughter are more bearable than overwhelming. It's not a quiet atmosphere, but it's not like sitting in a busy cafeteria.

My gaze wanders to a man sitting alone at the bar, and for a brief moment, my mind travels back to thoughts of Ben. How crazy would it be if he were sitting down to eat a meal here as well? The man shifts in his seat, and his profile is all wrong. I've tried to conjure up a full picture of him in my mind over the past weeks, but I'm not positive I'd even recognize him anymore. *I should have gotten his number.*

I groan, upset again with myself. And Darcy, even though I shouldn't be. She pulled me away from him, thinking she was helping me out. But if she had witnessed our chemistry, I think she would have encouraged me to stay. Shaking my head, I force myself out of my memories.

"Move on Kelly," I whisper to myself. He's long gone and it was a missed connection. Simple as that. Just as I end my mental pep talk, a man I recognize as Sam is walking toward me with a smile.

He's a handsome man—tall and slightly skinny. His blond hair is cut short and trimmed to perfection, and there's no facial hair to be seen. He's exactly what I would normally be attracted to.

"You must be Kelly," he says as stops next to the table.

"Sam, it's nice to meet you. Have a seat. I hope you don't mind that I didn't wait to get us one." I gesture to the chair opposite my own.

"Not at all. It's starting to get busy, so we might have had to wait awhile. Sorry I'm late." Sam pulls out the chair and folds himself into the seat.

"It's fine. I'm normally the one who's late. It's a nice change." We both chuckle and start to peruse the menu.

We exchange simple pleasantries, and after we order, we make small talk. We talk about our jobs—he works in HR for a mid-sized company that deals in e-commerce, and I don't spend much time talking about how unsatisfied I am with my job. It's not really something you bring up on a first date. Sam is lovely, and I'll admit he's easy to talk to. I'm enjoying myself.

A loud bark of laughter comes from the other side of the restaurant, and my gaze is pulled to the source—a table where four young men sit around it, laughing and having a good ole time. I catch one's profile, and I'm nearly struck dumb as Ben's face comes into focus in my mind. The man in question has nearly the same hairstyle and dark scruff on his face that sparked tingles down my spine at the bar. I rake my gaze down his arm and then zero in on the tattoo visible there. I can't make out the design, but shit—is that Ben? Desperately, I look at the rest of the table and notice a man to his right that looks like the guy Ben was at the club with. I can't remember his name. Garrett, Garth, Gary? Something like that.

I rack my brain for a way to casually get closer to the table without coming across as crazy to both my date and the table of men. I dart my eyes around the space and find that the restrooms are in the opposite direction of the table in question, and I deflate. It's going to either be a trip to crazy town or another missed connection.

A shadow descends over our table, pulling me out of my internal war. It's our server placing our food down in front of us. I give the server a distracted smile just as Sam says, "Wow, this looks amazing. Look at the size of these shrimp."

Pulled from my concern over Ben possibly being here, I force myself to focus on my date instead. *Wow, those are massive.* He ordered the seafood carbonara, which is a good pick, but I had a hankering for a red sauce pasta, so I went with the baked ziti.

Momentarily distracted by yummy food, I ask him, "So how do you know my cousin, Darcy?"

Sam coughs around the piece of shrimp he just put in his mouth, covers his mouth with his napkin, and clears his throat.

I give him a small smile. "I didn't mean to ask you a question right as you were taking a bite." He shakes his head as he pulls his hand away.

"No, you're fine. I'm just surprised she didn't tell you." He shifts in his seat as if uncomfortable. Immediately, my senses go on high alert. *Damn it, Darcy. What have you done?* Eyebrows raised, I urge him to share what Darcy didn't.

"Yeah, well, she works with my ex-girlfriend. I was

surprised she reached out to me to set up this date, to be honest. But I can't say I'm disappointed." He tries to give me a reassuring grin, but I just nod and chew on the inside of my cheek while I rework what he said.

Interesting. I wonder how close Darcy is to this ex of his. Clearly, not that close if she's setting him up with me.

Hesitantly, I ask, "How long have you been single?" I take a bite of my ziti.

"Umm, a couple of weeks." He winces.

My mouth falls open, then slams shut. "Wow. So this was fast." Quickly, I regroup. Maybe it wasn't a long relationship, so getting back into dating isn't a big deal for him. I don't want to pry, but I want to know.

"How long were you together?" My demeanor is still as I wait for his answer.

His face drops, and I can feel it. I just know I'm not going to like what I hear. "A little more than two years."

My eyes widen at his admittance. *Well, fuck me.*

I open my mouth to reply when a soft, unfamiliar voice cuts in.

"Sam, what are you doing here?"

I shut my mouth and look up to see a beautiful woman who looks slightly familiar, and that's when I realize this must be his ex. I've been to a few after-hours work events with Darcy, so it's highly probable we've been introduced. Right now, she's wearing a pretty, green, flowery dress. Her blonde hair is pulled up in a pony, and her eyes are filled with unshed tears.

She glances at me but pulls away quickly as if in fear I might attack. I look at Sam and wonder how I missed I was on a date with a lovesick puppy. He sits up straight in his chair, shoulders square like he's about to defend our date, when his eyes suddenly soften and his chin wobbles.

I fight off an eye roll and realize I'm about to witness

either some real sappy shit or another argument. *Damn, this public embarrassment is getting old.*

"Cass, what are you doing here?" He puffs out his chest, regaining a bit of his confidence.

"That's what I asked you, Sam," she whimpers.

At the risk of inserting myself into this confrontation, I say, "Excuse me, but do you just want to sit down and talk through this?" Neither Sam nor Cass pays any attention to me. Looks like I'm in it for the long haul. Leaning my elbow on the table, I cup my chin in my palm and watch the show.

"So, are you dating already?" Cass quivers.

"Yeah, I guess I am." Sam nods.

"Oh. It's a little soon, don't you think?"

"You broke up with me, remember Cass? I don't think you get a say in when I start dating." His chin juts out.

She hisses as if she's just been burnt by a flame, and that's when the big fat tears start to roll down her face.

As soon as she turns on the waterworks, I know Sam is done for.

"Cass, I'm sorry. This is just casual, I promise. Please don't cry."

I purse my lips. *Yup, I'm right here, guys.* I look around to see what kind of audience we have, and I'm thankful to find few people are paying attention. I also notice the table Ben sat at is now empty. Closing my eyes in defeat, I mentally kick myself for not getting up and risking embarrassment for the man I haven't been able to get off my mind for weeks. When I open them back up, Cass and Sam are having a hushed, but heated, conversation, so I find our server at the table next to us and signal that I need a to-go box. This ziti will still be damn good warmed up at home.

Several minutes later, I clear my throat and effectively get my date's attention. His eyes widen and he winces.

"Kelly, I'm so sorry." And, once again, before I can get anything out, Cass interrupts me.

"I'm leaving now. Bye, Sam." She rushes through the restaurant to the exit. I sigh, relieved this is over, but then I gear up for a heart-to-heart with dear ole Sam.

"Kelly, that was unexpected." He looks down, unable to meet my eyes.

"Yeah, it was. So that's your ex?" I try not to snort as I state the obvious.

"Yeah. Cass. I thought I was over her..." his voice trails.

"But you're not. And honestly, after a two-year relationship, how could you be? It hasn't been long since you two split." He shakes his head at my words, but I continue. "Sam, if it makes any difference, that woman is definitely not over you either."

He lifts his head, scrubbing a hand over his face. "Yeah?"

"You know what I think?" I offer. I'm ready to get out of here before I can bear witness to any more tears. Sam cocks his eyebrow. "I think you should go after her. Work things out. Get your happy ending with Cass."

His eyes gleam, and I swear tears will fall any minute. *Hold it together, man.*

"You're not mad?" He grimaces when he notices my food is all packed up and I'm ready to run.

"Nope." I pop the P, trying to show him I really couldn't care less. I mean, don't get me wrong, this sucks donkey balls, but what can I do? "Go get your girl."

He smiles and shakes himself out of his haze of emotion. He glances at the receipt, pulls out his wallet, and then throws down several dollars. "I'm so sorry you had to witness this, Kelly. And I'm sorry you didn't get a decent date. Thank you for being so cool, though." He rushes from our table and out of the restaurant.

The server walks by and gives me a remorseful look, and I shrug.

"It is what it is, man." I smile and he chuckles.

I get out of the restaurant and jump in an Uber, too mad to call up Darcy yet. I'll unleash my wrath on her when I get home. Instead, I shoot Aubrey a text.

ME: Remind me to never agree to a date set up by Darcy again.

Aubrey: Oh snap. Give me the deets. Now!

Me: My date is freshly single after a multi-year relationship. His ex showed up and they got into it.

Aubrey: What is it with you and entangled couples?

Me: It's a gift, really.

Aubrey: <Kourtney Kardashian true dat GIF>

Aubrey: What happened next? I'm on the edge of my seat.

Me: I told him to go get his girl back. After he cried…

Aubrey: Awe, you're so sweet. You'll forever be known as the woman who got them back together.

Me: Or the bitch who tried to steal her man.

Aubrey: Meh. Maybe.

Aubrey: Come stay with us this weekend. The surf cast is on point and you deserve a break.

Me: Pull my arm, why don't ya.

Me: I'll be there.

Aubrey: Sweet. I've got someone I want you to meet.

Me: Wait. Noooo.

Me: You can't do this to me!!!

Aubrey: <evil laugh GIF> JK, hon. JK

. . .

MY HEARTBEAT SLOWS NOW that I know she was kidding. But hot damn, I don't think I can take another date like tonight. I think I'll hold off a few weeks before going on any more dates. I need to get out of whatever funk I'm currently in.

With a few minutes to go until I'm back home, I think about how I'm going to ream out my darling cousin for this shitty blind date. What the hell was she thinking? What the hell was I thinking going through with it?

FIVE

Ben
———

I pull the wetsuit up my body and stuff my arms inside. I take a deep breath, and I can taste the briny air wafting in from the ocean. Once I'm snug, I turn and grab my board. Being born and raised in Chicago, surfing isn't second nature to me. I'm actually quite terrible, if I'm being honest. I never played sports—I was always too busy kicking ass at video games—but surfing is a challenge I quite enjoy. I'm not sure I'll ever be any good at it, but as long as I'm having fun, I'll keep trying it while I'm in Cali.

I walk beside Garland toward the water that's lapping onto the sand with each incoming wave, the soft glow of the sun peeking up from the horizon. The boardwalk behind me is lined with food and shop vendors, but most are still closed and won't open for another couple of hours. I'm not normally up this early, but I had the morning off and I head back home tomorrow. Garland promised a morning of surfing this trip.

"The waves are clean," he says as we watch the water. "I'm amped."

"Yeah, you've never brought me to this beach before. It

looks like a good one," I say as I notice there are several surfers already out. Luckily, it's not busy at all.

"Hermosa Beach is my new go-to. I don't mind the forty-five minute drive from the city when the waves are great and the beach isn't crowded." He nods to the shore.

"These waves are going to kick my ass. I can feel it." I chuckle. They'll kick my ass, but I don't really care. Maybe the experience will even make me a little better.

Garland snorts in agreement. "Hell yeah, they are. But what do you expect, ya kook?"

I shake my head. "Why is it as soon as you step foot onto the beach, you immediately start speaking in surf slang?"

He thumps me on the shoulder. "It's the way of the surfer, bro." The way he says bro is stereotypical, high-as-a-kite surfer dude.

We paddle out a solid thirty feet and wait a few beats for the next wave to roll. After we catch it, we settle back in and repeat the cycle over and over until I've had my fill.

What seems like hours later, I drag myself out of the swell and plop down on the beach. I have no idea how much time has passed, but normally, I can only handle about an hour. The water is cold this early in the year, but it's not a turnoff. Garland will probably surf for a bit longer, though he won't surf as long as he normally would because he'll feel bad I'm sitting here waiting. I don't mind, though. Part of the reason I like being out here is that it provides much needed time away from my phone and all things gaming. The crash of the waves and the fizz of the foam as it sweeps ashore lolls me into a relaxing state as my body comes down from the high from riding the waves. A soft breeze ruffles through my ocean-soaked hair.

I watch Garland and some other surfers. There's one in particular that's kicking butt out there. At one point, I realize the surfer is a girl, and I'm immoderately drawn to her. She's damn good. If I knew more about surfing, I'd be able to identify some of the tricks she's doing, but I'm still a novice. I don't recall when Garland joins me because I can't take my eyes off her.

"Do you know who that is?" I ask him.

"Not from this far away. She's probably a pro. She's done some high-level shit." We both watch in awe. It's not long before she paddles back to the shore.

"Dude, you've got a hard-on for the surfer girl." Garland laughs as we stand.

"What?" I glance down in horror before realizing he's just being a dick. I punch him in the arm. "Grow up, asshole."

He's still chuckling as we turn to head back to his Jeep. But I can't help that my feet move slow. I want the surfer girl to catch up. Hell, I don't know why. She could be jail bait, for all I know. I'm closer to thirty than I am to twenty, so I don't need to be drooling over some baby surfer.

We make it to the parking lot and strip out of our surf suits. We still have our trunks on underneath—we wouldn't want to put on a show. Something out of the corner of my eye gets my attention. I look to the car a few spots down when I see it's the girl from the waves. Focusing on her, I can tell she's in her twenties, and I sigh a breath of relief. She wears her long-sleeved surf suit that fits like a one-piece bathing suit. Her toned, tan legs go on for days, the skintight fabric of the suit doing nothing to hide her full, perfect tits and lean stomach. She leans her board up against the car and reaches to pull out her topknot. Dark hair falls past her shoulders as she shakes it out. I'm transfixed by her motions as she runs her fingers through her long locks.

"Shit, man. Are you drooling?"

I startle at Garland's words. "Fuck," I snarl, trying to focus on my task of getting my board in Garland's back seat. He laughs from the other side of the car as he secures his board to the top, the tail end of the board hanging out the trunk window.

My eyes track her moves, and when she turns toward me, I'm nearly struck dumb. Is that the girl from Club Punch?

No way.

I study her face as my heart soars. I never thought I'd see her again, but here she is right in front of me. I didn't think it was possible, but knowing she's a badass surfer chick and seeing the way her wetsuit molds to her skin has me that much hotter for her. If only she would look at me.

As if she hears my plea, her eyes catch mine. Her brows furrow and then she looks away. While I realize I've been caught staring, I want her to look at me again. She goes about her business, pretending she didn't just catch a stranger staring her down. But then she glances over her shoulder at me. She bites her lip as if she's not sure how to feel about the fact I'm not breaking eye contact.

"Dude, really? Take a picture, it'll last longer." Garland leans his forearms on his car door, grinning like a fool.

"I think it's the girl from Club Punch," I tell him, finally taking my eyes off her.

"From last month? Really?" He keeps his cool and casually looks her way. "How crazy would that be?"

Kelly climbs in her car, the door shutting behind her, and I blow out a deep breath, silently kicking myself for not going over there. But then her car door swings open, and she steps back out of the car. Trying to save face, I quickly pull my attention away from her when I realize she's walking toward us. *Shit. I'm a creeper.*

I finish sliding my board into the open back seat when I hear, "Ben?"

Awareness tingles up my spine. I answer her questioning tone with a massive grin. "Kelly."

"Oh my God, I thought that was you." She stops a few feet away from me, and I want to pull her in for a hug. But I don't because I'm still trying to blow off the creep factor I had going.

"Yeah, I saw you at your car and did a double-take." I chuckle while Garland sputters a "Holy shit" from the other side of the car.

"So crazy that you're here. Do you normally surf this beach?" Her smiling face is utterly gorgeous. Her hair is drying in the sun, and it's already starting to get those sexy beach waves. Damn, I bet it will smell like salty ocean water for the rest of the day. Her round, grass-green eyes sparkling in delight causes my heart to slam in my chest. She's just as happy to see me as I am her.

"First time. Garland comes here, though." I nod toward Garland.

"Sup?" He juts his chin.

"Garland, that's right. I knew you had a good name." She directs her smile and a sing-song laugh his way, and I narrow my eyes at him. He better not hijack this conversation.

Garland's chest puffs up, and I groan. "It *is* a very good name," he boasts.

"Talk about a small world, huh? What are the chances of us meeting again?" I pull her attention back to me.

"It's really crazy. Actually, I thought I saw you the other night at Luigi's Italiano. You weren't there, were you?"

"Shit, I was. Why didn't you say anything?" I'm immediately bummed I could have more time with her.

She blushes. "Uh, I was on a date." She wrings her fingers, clearly nervous with her response.

Well, damn, she's in a relationship. My hopes plummet off a cliff realizing the chemistry between us was meant to be a one-time thing. I'm not the kind of dude that messes with a taken woman.

"Ah, that makes sense. Either way, it was great to see you, Kelly. You're a kick-ass surfer. I'm impressed. I couldn't stop watching you out there," I say.

Turning away from her, I catch Garland's eye, and he's smashing his lips together. Then he shifts his head toward her and mouths, "Ask her out." I glare at him and give a tight shake. Clearly, he didn't catch on to the whole boyfriend thing.

"Thanks. I've been surfing since I was little. If I could grow fins, I'd live in the ocean." She chuckles. While I'd love more time with her, I'm ready to leave. I don't want to flirt with someone else's girlfriend.

I laugh at her reply and try to nicely end the conversation. "Well, like I said—"

"Do you want to get breakfast with us?" Garland buts in. "We're about to head to Joe's Diner a few blocks away. You should join us." He ignores my glare. I plaster on a grin when I turn back to Kelly, and her questioning glance tells me my behavior hasn't gone unnoticed.

"Uh. I mean, I could eat. Would that be okay with you, Ben?" She puts the decision back on me. *Shit, I'm not an asshole.*

I shrug. "Yeah, that's cool." I feel like a douche, but the idea of her having a boyfriend irks me.

Her smile wavers for a second before she nods and tells us she'll meet us there. She heads back to her car, and I climb into the Jeep before punching Garland in the shoulder.

"Fuck, what was that for?" he whines.

"She has a boyfriend," I growl.

"She didn't say that." He pushes the ignition button and the Jeep rattles to life.

"She said she was on a date."

"That doesn't translate into having a boyfriend. It's a modern world, my friend. Women date just for fun all the time, if you know what I mean." He waggles his eyebrows with a chuckle as he pulls out of the parking lot. "Look, you've had a hard-on for her since the club."

I open my mouth to rebuke when he continues, "Nuh-uh, buddy. Remember when you thought you saw her on the street the other day? And man, you were drooling so hard back there before she walked over. You've got it bad. I'm just helping a brother out." His cocky grin is full of shit. "You'll thank me later."

I shake my head as I look out the side mirror, seeing Kelly's tiny sedan following behind us. Then I catch the deep-set frown on my face and try to relax my features. I want to spend time with her. I just don't want to get to know her if she's already attached to someone else. I'm not into long-distance relationships, and seeing as I'm not in Cali on the regular, it doesn't make sense for me to get to know a chick for just friendship. Maybe more of a friend with benefits kind of thing. All right, maybe I *am* an asshole.

We pull into the diner and Kelly parks in the back of the lot, but she doesn't get out of her car right away.

"Why don't you go in and get a table? I'll wait for Kelly," I say, and Garland winks at me and heads into Joe's. I lean up against his Jeep, wondering what's taking Kelly so long. Maybe she's regretting her decision to come after all. I squint and see her moving around in her car, then her horn sets off in a long honk. *What the...*

I push off the Jeep and walk toward her car. Just as I get close enough to reach out and touch the vehicle, her door pops open. A naked foot juts out and she drops a pair of leather sandals on the ground. Her other leg appears, and I glimpse a very high part of her thigh just as she yanks down the skirt of a short, soft-looking dress. *Ah, so she was changing.*

I smirk. She jumps when she sees me standing there. "Shit, I didn't know you were there." Her face reddens. "How long have you been there?"

I know what she's asking, and I don't hide the slow grin that covers my face. She must think I got an eyeful because the soft shade of red on her cheeks cranks up a notch. I chuckle and put her at ease. "I headed over after hearing the horn."

She sighs. "Oh, good. I didn't think about the fact I was still in my surf suit when I agreed to breakfast, so I had to change in my car." She looks up at me from her seat, and I reach out my hand to help her out. She takes it, and a jolt of electricity shoots up my arm at the connection. She smiles and grips my hand harder as she raises from the car. I pull her and it has her standing right in front of me. Toe to toe, chest to chest.

"Hi," I say, pulling my stare away from her lips to look in her eyes.

"Hi." Her voice is breathy and soft. Then her stomach grumbles, and I chuckle. "Let's get some food."

I turn, still holding her hand, and gently yank her behind me before letting her hand drop. We find Garland at a booth, sitting smack in the middle of one side. I slide into the opposite side and Kelly follows suit.

"I was beginning to worry." Garland smiles.

"I had to change. It wasn't an easy feat in the car." She giggles, and Garland gives her a cheesy smile in return.

While I know deep down he would never go after a girl I'm into, I want to punch him for the grin.

I look down at my menu and try to decide what to order. When Kelly orders the Surfer's Deluxe, I'm reminded how she had no qualms about eating all the fried goodness I ordered at the club. I'm impressed that a tiny thing like her can consume all that food.

"Make that two," Garland tells our server. "Surfing makes me hungry. Eggs, bacon, hash browns, hotcakes, and biscuits and gravy is really calling to me." He hands over his menu.

"I hear ya!" Kelly adds.

"So, Kelly, you live here in Hermosa?" Garland asks. It's not lost on me that he's the one making small talk.

"No, I live in Culver City. My best friend and her husband live here, and I visit them on the weekends. I mostly come to surf, but I enjoy time with my girl." She toys with the straw in her glass of OJ while she talks.

"Nice. We're in Culver, too," he replies, "Well, it's where I live and work, that is." He raises an eyebrow at me. I can feel Kelly's questioning stare, but I just grunt and take a drink of my coffee. Garland shakes his head but continues his interrogation.

"What do you do?" he asks her.

"I work at an accounting firm. It's on the main stretch. You?" she volleys back.

"We work at Lasso. It's right there, too." He sits back with a huge shit-eating grin on his face. "Talk about a small world. We probably get our coffee at the same café." In unison, they both say, "The Melting Moon." And then they laugh before Garland's face slackens. "Holy shit. I know why you look familiar."

I perk up, and she cocks her head, waiting for his reason.

"About a month ago, there was a couple at the Moon. They were fighting and a woman fell into them. That was you, wasn't it?" I slide my attention toward her, and she hangs her head and sighs. When she lifts her head, she isn't blushing, but grinning.

"Ugh, what are the chances you'd be there to witness that?" she asks.

"It was the highlight of our day. You remember that, Ben?"

Nodding, I say, "Yeah, I'm sorry that happened to you." I chew on my lip, thinking back through our encounters. I twist my lip to fight a smile before asking, "How does a girl like you—always tripping into people—glide so gracefully through the water?"

Garland hoots. Kelly scrunches her nose in mock offense, then laughs before answering. "Honestly, I have no idea why I'm so damn clumsy sometimes."

Just as our food is placed in front of us, I laugh and lean in to bump her shoulder, letting her know I'm just joshing her.

We dig into our meals, causing the conversation to slow for all of about five minutes before Garland throws me under the bus.

"So, Kel—can I call you Kel? I need to clear the air." He leans back, placing his fork next to his stack of fluffy pancakes.

"Only if I can call you Gar," she replies deadpan.

"I'll allow it." He nods. "Do you have a boyfriend?"

I hold my breath while I wait for her to answer.

"Uh, well, I appreciate your forwardness. I do not." She grins.

Pushing air out my nose, I mask my relief by taking a sip of coffee.

Garland's smugness clouds my vision. "I don't know if

you've noticed, but my boy, Ben, has been a bit grumpy thinking you're already spoken for."

My mouth drops where it hangs while I gather my thoughts. Snapping it shut, I hiss, "Spoken for? What century do you live in, man?"

"Hardy har. I call it like it is. Now the air is clear, and it smells like teen spirit. You're welcome."

I grumble while Kelly bumps me with her shoulder. "It's because I mentioned the date, wasn't it?" she asks. I shift my head and catch her gorgeous smile light up her face. "It was a blind date, and he ended up running after his ex-girlfriend in hopes of winning her back."

Suddenly, I feel overprotective and angry. Why are people always putting this woman in awkward situations?

"I… Wow, I'm sorry to hear your date sucked. But, I'm also glad it did." I squint at my own words and she giggles. The sound is melodic, and I would do anything to hear the sound again.

"So now we've gotten that out of the way, no more grumpy Ben," she says, making a pouty face. I have the urge to wrap my arm around her and pull her into my side, but I refrain.

"No more grumpy Ben," I repeat mockingly. I hear a snort from the peanut gallery.

Our food demands our attention again, but as we push plates away from our stuffed stomachs, she hits me with the questions I avoided earlier.

"You never answered. Do you live in Culver City? You work at Lasso, right?" She shifts her body toward me, giving me her full attention.

"I'm on a contracting job with Lasso. I actually live in Chicago." I hold my gaze, waiting for the disappointment to come when she finds I'm not local.

Her eyes widen. "Chicago. Wow." There it is.

"Dude, tell her about your day job," Garland interjects.

"Yeah, tell me," she heckles me.

"I'm a professional gamer." Per usual, confusion sets in on her face. "As in video games. I compete in team and solo tournaments. Mostly Call of Battle, but a handful of others, too."

She chews her lip. "Interesting."

"Ben 'Fortify' Ford is one of the top players in the world right now," Garland brags on my behalf. In the video game industry, it's a big fucking deal, but right now, in this moment, it's not.

"Yeah," I murmur. My heart plummets deep into my gut. This is a normal response when I tell people what I do. Up next is some shitty comment about me not having a "real job."

"I didn't even know that was a career. That's really cool. But then, that's coming from a girl who has no idea what the hell I want to do with my own career. What is it you're doing with Lasso?"

I'm momentarily stunned at her words but recover quickly. "Voice-overs for video games."

"Ohhh, that's fun." Then her eyes light up. "I bet you'd make one hell of a narrator for romance books."

Garland chokes on his drink, and I snort. "Really?"

Her expression turns serious "Oh my God, yes! If you have a sexy enough voice to make women's favorite book boyfriends come to life in their ears, readers would pay you to read the damn phone book."

I chuckle at how serious she is. "Well, maybe I'll look into it."

The plates are cleared soon after, and Kelly peers down at her phone. "Oh, shit. I've gotta get going." She looks sad, and I can't blame her. I'm not thrilled our time is coming to an end.

"Oh, yeah. Right," I mumble, sliding out of the booth.

"I need to pay for my meal first." She sounds dejected.

"No way. I've got it covered." I smile and she returns it, but I can't help noticing she looks a little sad.

I slide out of the booth and she follows. As I turn to slide back in, Garland's eyes are about to bulge out of his head. He mouths vehemently, "Number! Get her number!" And I nod.

"Kelly, can I have your number?" It just sputters from my mouth like an assault of words. *Smooth, man. Real smooth.*

Relief fills her eyes, and a playful smile dances across her lips. "I honestly thought you were gonna let me go again without asking."

Tossing my hands up, I say, "In my defense, I thought you were coming back at the club. I thought I had time."

She clucks her tongue. "Touché." She holds out her hand in a *give me* manner. "I'll put it in your phone."

I reach into my pocket for my phone and come up empty-handed. Trying the other pocket, I mumble a fuck. "It's in the car."

She chortles, and fucking Garland Thorpe smacks his head with his hand and mutters, "You've got to be kidding me."

"Here." She leans over the table and grabs a napkin from the dispenser and digs out a sharpie from her tiny purse. "I've never written my number on a napkin before, so consider yourself a lucky guy." She slides her digits toward me, and I tap my index finger on the napkin.

"This is going in my phone as soon as I'm back in the car."

She gives me one last sexy-as-sin smile. "I hope you do." Then she waves and walks away.

"Fuck, you're a hot mess for this woman, bro."

Garland shakes his head while the server drops the bill off at our table.

"I got this, you asshat," I mumble, but he reaches across the table to snag the receipt out of my hand.

"It's all on me, remember? Business." His tone's annoyed.

"There was nothing business about this meal. Plus, I'm paying for Kelly's meal." I jerk the black receipt book away from him, and his hand drops, knocking over my half-empty glass of water.

"Shit," we both cringe. Alarm erupts from my body as the napkin with Kelly's phone number soaks up most of the water.

"Fuuuckk." I snag the soggy paper and hold it up, far from the table. A massive black hole takes root in my gut as I see the last four digits have morphed into blurred black marks.

"What are the chances, man?" Garland sits back in his seat, staring at the destroyed napkin in as much disappointed shock as I am.

Was this a fucking sign from the universe, or what?

SIX

Kelly

He never called.

Not the day we had breakfast. Not in the days after, either. No, it's been two weeks and Ben still hasn't called. The disappointment hangs over me like a sad, grumpy storm cloud. It reminds me that this isn't the first time I've felt disappointed over a guy I don't even know.

I gave him my number, though. I wrote it on a freaking napkin. I must have gotten the wrong impression when I thought he was into me. I guess I was wrong.

I drum my fingers on my desk, my chin in my palm as I stare out the window near my cubical. The tall walls that encase my cubical have always allowed me privacy to daydream, but if I leave the sliding door open, I can get a fantastic view of busy Culver City.

A soft ding from my computer alerts me to a private message in our company messaging system, effectively tearing me away from my thoughts of being a fool.

It was a message from another admin assistant reminding me that the rest of the admins are treating me to lunch on my last day here at Hill House Accounting.

The weekend I met up with Ben in Hermosa Beach, Aubrey asked me to come work with her at Pawsitively Pixy Animal Haven, her animal shelter. She started the shelter a couple of years ago, and it's been a wild success. But her manager is going on maternity leave, and she needs someone to fill in temporarily.

With Aubrey, I've never been shy about sharing my feelings regarding my distaste for my current job. In return, she's been honest in how she wants me to move to Hermosa. It took me the weekend, but by the time I was heading back to the city, I was planning all the things I needed to do to quit my job and move my life to the beach.

Honestly, it didn't take Aubrey long to convince me to move. I love animals. And while I'm used to working corporate office jobs, the idea of working in a nonprofit shelter seems like a welcome break in the monotonous day-to-day I'm currently used to. Plus, if I take my work home, it's probably going to be furry with four legs. Who can say no to that?

I've never actually been one to desire climbing the corporate ladder, so it's not like I'm leaving behind a career I've been working toward. It feels like the right move in all the ways that matter.

Darcy is sad I'm moving out, but honestly, I need a break from my party-going cousin. I love her dearly, but I want my own place. And Aubrey and Chance just happen to have an apartment over their detached garage, which they're letting me rent.

Every time I've started a new chapter with a new job, I've hoped I'd enjoy it more than the chapter before. And I've always wound up slightly disappointed. But this time, I'm genuinely excited to move to the beach and have more surf and bestie time. Plus, I really am looking forward to my new gig—even if it's temporary.

My private message pings again to ask what kind of sandwich I want from my favorite sandwich shop down the block, and I type out a quick response.

I have an exit interview with HR and Mr. Bales shortly after lunch, and I'm not looking forward to it. Mostly because I know Mr. Bales doesn't understand the sudden resignation. So, while this day is supposed to be bittersweet, it's sweeter than anything else at the moment. Thank goodness for the lunch with a few of my colleagues I actually enjoyed working with.

But, hey, at least I get a free meal. *I got a free meal out of Ben as well.*

Blinking rapidly, annoyed my mind found a way to think about the dark-haired, tatted-up gamer. I was so excited when I realized the man at the beach was the same man from the Club. Spending the next hour with him and learning more about him was fascinating. I didn't want to leave him, but once again, I did. I thought it was fate that brought us back together. Maybe I was wrong.

I SHUT MY DOOR GENTLY, locking it before skipping down the wooden staircase from my apartment leading to the driveway. I don't want to wake any of the neighbors with slamming doors and my overall excitement on my first morning of only living minutes from the beach. It's early, but I have a date with the waves.

Jumping the final step, I skid to a stop when I see Aubrey and Chance's small, shaggy-haired goat, Pixy, standing in the grass next to my car. He's chewing on grass, and he's without his normal leash, so I wonder if he escaped. I scan the yard for Aubrey or Chance, and I don't see them. It looks like I'll need to herd Pixy back home before I can leave.

"Hey, little guy," I say just above a whisper, careful not to spook him. I reach my hand out and take a small step toward him. He takes a slow, methodical chew of the grass hanging out of his mouth, staring me down in the early morning darkness.

This goat and I know each other well, but even so, I don't want to make any sudden movements and send him running.

"How'd you get out here, Pix?" I ask, slowly advancing toward him.

Aubrey and Chance have had him for years, and really, this goat is a part of their great love story. I've never been one to think of a goat as a pet, but Pixy here is well-loved and has an easy life for sure.

A door slams somewhere down the sleepy street, and I jump, not expecting the noise. "Shit," I sputter, taking a full step toward the goat.

Then I see it happen. Pixy's muscles freeze up, and he tips over with a thud in the grass.

Shit, shit, shit.

Hurrying toward him, I do my best to calm my erratic breathing. This is what Pixy does when he gets nervous. It's an actual genetic disorder called fainting goat, or so Aubrey tells me. His fainting spell shouldn't last long, but I feel terrible I scared him.

"What the hell happened?" comes a deep, familiar voice. My head shoots up, and I spot Chance walking around the side of the house toward me and the passed-out Pixy. There's humor laced in his questioning tone, so I sigh in relief just as Pixy's statue-like body starts to relax.

"He didn't seem startled to see me, but then there was a noise down the street. I jumped, then he did his thing and fainted." I bit my lip, staring down as the goat springs up. With a flick of his tail, he goes back to his morning grazing.

Chance chuckles as he comes to a stop next to Pixy. "Don't worry about it, Kel. See, he's fine."

"I don't care how normal it is. I will never not be worried about him every time he tips over stiff as a board." Shaking my head, I reach down and scratch behind his ear.

"I get it." He nods. Chance is a great guy, and I'm happy he and Aubrey worked out their shit and got their happily ever after. Their love story is novel-worthy, to say the least, and it's one I love hearing about over and over. Even if it involved them putting me in the middle of some very uncomfortable conversations.

I take a step away from the two most important beings in Aubrey's life. I need to get to the beach. "I'm glad he wasn't out here alone. I thought he escaped."

"Nope, I'm out here with him. I was in the garage. Inspiration hit me early this morning. But thanks for checking on him. You heading to the beach?" He stuffed his hands in the pockets of his jersey basketball shorts. Chance used to play professional soccer back in Australia. Now, he spends his days as an artist, using junk to make stunning artwork.

"You know it." I shoot him a smile and turn to get into my car.

"You know you'll never leave Hermosa now, right? You've fallen under its spell."

A laugh bubbles up my throat. "Oh yeah? How so?" I open my door and look at him over my car.

"Besides living on the best beach in the state, you'll be able to get up early and hit the waves every morning. What more could a surfer want from life?" His words ring true. "You'll never want to leave."

I snicker. "I think you're probably right, Chance. I'll see you later." I wave goodbye and head to the beach.

After a couple of hours in the ocean, I head home and do some unpacking before heading over to Aubrey's for dinner. I've made it clear to her that, while I'm living over their garage, I'm not living *with* them. It's not Aubrey's responsibility to take care of me. I pay rent and I have a tiny kitchen in my apartment, so it's not on her to feed me. Really, the apartment is perfect. It's small, but it features a bedroom, open concept living area, eat-in kitchen, and bathroom. There is even a tiny closet with a washer and dryer hooked up. But I did promise I'd come over for dinner at least once a week.

"So, how were the waves this morning?" Aubrey asks as she flits around her spacious kitchen.

"A little choppy but manageable." I slide into one of the stools at the island bar.

"You want a glass of wine?" she asks, pulling a glass out of the cabinet.

"Do you have any of that blueberry wine?" I ask. I'm not a huge wine drinker, but I love me some fruity stuff.

"Of course I do. Do you think I wouldn't stock up on that stuff with you moving in?" Her grin is huge as she pours me a massive glass.

"Whoa, I'll be nursing that all night." I reach out, covering the top of the glass with my hand.

"You don't have to drive, so enjoy it." She cackles.

I shake my head at her antics and take a sip. Crisp, cold sweetness hits my tongue, and my eyes flutter shut. Okay, maybe I'll drink this up sooner than expected. It's so damn good.

"I'm excited to show you the ropes tomorrow. Liz still

has a week before she's out on maternity leave, so you'll work with her closely this week. Take in whatever you can. Anything that comes up after she leaves, I can help with," she says, setting the timer on the oven after shoving in a pan of lasagna.

"Good. I'm excited, too. Kind of nervous, but overall, excited," I tell her while I watch her slather butter over big, thickly cut slices of Texas toast.

"You're going to love it. Unlike your co-workers at Hill House, you'll enjoy the people you're working with. Plus, your boss is amazing." She bobbles her head and giggles.

I join her. "Yeah, but I heard she's a little cray-cray."

"You heard right," Chance says as he walks into the kitchen. Walking right over to Aubrey, he lays a tender kiss to her temple. "But, we still love her," he adds as he pulls away.

She rolls her eyes playfully as Chance heads to the fridge and pulls out a beer.

"I can handle a little crazy." I laugh at the two of them.

"Really, though," he says as he walks back the way he came. "Aubrey has done something great with that shelter. You're going to love working there." He winks at her, shoots me a smile, and saunters back into the living room where there are cheers in response to a game of some kind. I'm going to guess soccer.

"All right, so you've got the apartment, you've got the waves, and you've got the job. The next up on my *Kelly's New Chapter* checklist is to find a man. What's your plan with that one?" Aubrey sings sweetly.

I sputter and cover my mouth so the wine I just drank doesn't come spitting out all over the delicious-looking garlic bread. "I'm sorry what?"

"You need a man. How do you plan to find one?" she repeats.

"First of all, I don't need a man," I grouch.

"Okay, bad wording. You need sex, yeah? And you wouldn't mind some loving and romantic dates, right?" She waggles her eyebrows.

"Remind me why I tell you anything about my dating life," I mumble around another drink.

"What dating life do you speak of? The date you went on with the guy who still had the hots for his ex? Or the mystery dude you've met twice but is too much of a coward to call you?" She levels me with a *you know I'm right* stare.

I glare at her and sigh. "Fine. You're right. I have no dating life."

"So, when you're ready, I'll help you." She shrugs, turning to put the tray of garlic toast on the stovetop of the heated oven.

I snort. "I think I'm gonna chill for a bit. The last one really messed with my head."

She cocks her head. "Kelly, you don't even know him. And is one semi-breakfast date enough to mess with your head?" Her eyes soften. "Was it really enough?"

Sighing, I tell her the truth. "I feel stupid for saying yes to that question, but it's the truth. There was so much chemistry between us at the bar, and missing out on seeing how hot that chemistry could have been was a bummer. But I didn't even know his name at the time, so I moved on. But then, I kept seeing him—or thinking I saw him— like the universe was dangling our missed connection right in front of me. But meeting up with him on the beach was an eerily fated random chance, you know? The chemistry was still there. He got grouchy when he thought I had a boyfriend, and honestly, I really don't think I misinterpreted what was brewing between us. I gave him my number, but he didn't call. It stings. It feels like he was the one that got away."

Aubrey's eyes are full of pity, and I fight back the urge to roll my eyes at her.

"Don't pity me. I'll get over it—him. Because you're right, I don't even know him. I know where he's from, what he does, his name, and where he works in Culver City. I don't actually know the guy."

Her eyes flash with excitement, and I narrow my own at her change of tone. "If you know all that basic, but specific, stuff about him, why don't you do some digging and find him?"

I shake my head and sputter, "Because I gave him *my* number."

"A woman is perfectly capable of making the first move, girlfriend." She tsks, wagging a finger at me. "Admit it, you're too scared to make the first move."

Licking my lips, I fire back, "Isn't the fact that I gave him my number indeed the first move?"

"Nope. Making the next connection is." She crosses her arms over her chest, staring me down.

I don't break eye contact with the slightly overbearing woman I call a best friend. She doesn't back down from our stare-off. Her deliberately raised eyebrows and the titling of her head finally cause me to sigh.

"Fine. You win. Maybe, just maybe, I was hoping the universe would make this thing," I twirl my finger in the air, "work on its own. Plus, he's not even local. That's a pretty big issue to overcome."

"So, what you're saying is you just wanted to put all the hard work on the universe, and if it was meant to happen, it just... would?" Her nose wrinkles.

I shift in my seat. "Yeah," I squeak. At her words, my face and neck grow hot, and I have an overwhelming need to hide my face.

She nods slowly. "Right, but you know, nothing worth having in life just lands in your lap, yeah? And if it does, it's not going to stay there without you putting some effort and work into it. Especially relationships. Those things are harder than anything else, but they also offer the most reward. If you're so caught up in this guy that the *universe*," she air quotes the word, "dangled in front of you, then put in the time and figure out if it can be something real."

Biting my lip, I mull over her words. "I know you're right, but have you thought about the fact that it's been two weeks and he hasn't called? Will I look like a fool if I track him down and reach out and he's not interested?" My words are tense, my adrenaline picking up with the thought of the unnecessary embarrassment that situation could cause.

"Okay, I hear you. And I understand what you're saying." Her words are kind, soothing. "What if you just track him down? Find out more about this guy and then you can decide if it's worth the risk. Maybe he's not what he seems? Maybe you find his Instagram and it's full of shady, creepy shit. Like he posts pictures of plastic bags in the street, or maybe he's a player and posts pictures of different chicks every day."

I snort out a giggle. "Is the only possible outcome that he's a creep?"

Her smile widens. "No, the other outcome is that he's exactly what he's presented himself as, and you decide to risk it and call him."

Pressing my lips together, I weigh my options. If I find him, I don't necessarily have to contact him. But at least I'll have found him, right? I'll have done my due diligence.

"Fine. I'll find him." I say in a whisper.

"Correction—we will find him." She reaches over and squeezes my hand. "You drink, I'll get my laptop." She hurries out of the room, and I do what she demanded and gulp down my wine.

She's back in a blink of an eye, and she shimmies onto the plush stool next to me. Opening up her laptop, she asks, "Okay, let's do this. Do you know his full name?"

"Yeah, it's Ben Ford, I think," I tell her, and her eyebrow raises. "No, I'm positive. His friend said his full name but called him by a nickname, too." I close my eyes and try to think back. "Ben 'Fortify' Ford is what he said." My eyes snap open.

"Hmm. Okay. And you said he's in Chicago?" She types his name into Goggle.

"Yes, he's a professional gamer."

"Ah, yes. Strange profession but interesting, for sure." She hits enter, and within a nanosecond, the page produces results.

"Bingo. Looky here! The first result is about Team NoMad and there's his name." Her mouse hovers over the link, then she clicks. The page that populates is some kind of official gaming league with stats and schedules. We quickly find his team's name at the top of the list. After a few more clicks, we end up on Team NoMad's homepage.

Aubrey clicks on the members' page, and as the page loads, my belly fills with butterflies. There's a professional group photo on the screen, and I zero in on the handsome man I'm looking for.

"Shit, those are some attractive people," Aubrey hums. I scan the picture and agree, but my eyes are drawn back to Ben. His messy black hair and dark eyes and cocky grin capture my attention. He stands at the end, his arms crossed and the sleeves of his shirt pushed up on his forearms. All those mesmerizing tattoos cover his arms, and my mouth starts to salivate.

"Which one is Ben?" Aubrey startles me with her question.

"The one on the end." I point.

"Damn, girl, you into bad boys now?" Her tone is mixed with shock and awe.

"I don't think his looks match his personality. Does he have a profile or something?" I ask, the urge to find out more about this man growing by the second.

She scrolls and clicks and the page loads. A larger picture, clearly from the same shoot, fills the screen, and a bio populates on one side.

I scan the details my mind is hungry for as Aubrey lets out a sigh. "I'm not gonna lie, I'd be hung up on him, too. He's fucking hot."

"I heard that," yells Chance from the other room.

"Babe, you're the only man for me, and I'll never be more attracted to anyone else than I am to you," she reassures her husband.

She lowers her voice this time. "I get it now, girl. I absolutely do."

I lean into her and nudge her shoulder with my own and grin. "Do you see any kind of contact info?"

"Oh, yeah, looks like this links to a Twitter account. But it says if you want to contact him, you should email their manager."

I bite my lip. Of course, I wasn't expecting a personal email or phone number plastered on the Internet for the world to access, but I don't want to reach out via a middleman or on social media.

"Let's have a look-see at what Benny Boy tweets about," Aubrey mummers conspiratorially. I chuckle, remembering his response to that nickname at Club Punch.

We scroll through his Twitter feed and find that it's all

just game related. So basically, it's a foreign language to me. Aubrey must agree because she sighs.

"I don't know what a lot of this means, but he doesn't seem like a creeper. He's got nearly two million followers. His interactions with others aren't douchey. Cocky sometimes, yes, but he doesn't come across as a tool." She scrolls through more tweets.

"I'm so relieved," I snarl, not even bothering to hide my sarcasm.

"You should be." She chuckles. She clicks back to his profile, leans over the island, and grabs the notepad and pen tucked under the lip of the bar. She scribbles something on the note and hands it to me. "Here's his Twitter handle and his manager's email. Do what you want with it; contact him or don't. I won't push you, but at least you have this info."

I take the small sheet of paper and stare at it before nodding. I fold it in half and shove it in my pocket.

A mix of emotions battles it out in my mind. Seeing him again, even just a picture, has ignited all kinds of feelings within me. But the hesitancy I still have about reaching out at this point clouds my mind. I honestly don't know what I'll do. If only I could get another sign from the universe.

SEVEN

Ben

At the sound of a ding, a flight attendant announces we can remove our seat belts. I do just that, then lean forward and dig out my headphones and phone from my backpack. I push back into my seat, trying to get comfortable for the nearly four-hour trip to Cali.

It's been a month since my last visit, and I'm itching to head back. I'd be amiss if I didn't admit to myself that part of the reason for wanting to be back in Cali was Kelly. I think it's too much to ask the universe to give me one last chance to meet up with her and get things right, but damn if I'm not hoping it happens. I rest my elbow on the armrest while I swipe through my Spotify playlists when I bump into the arm already resting there.

"Sorry, Bern," I mumble and move my arm, looking over to my teammate, Bernie.

"No worries." She smiles as she turns on her Kindle. The image of a naked man, with a shirt hanging around his chest fills the screen. What the hell is she reading?

Normally, I travel to Cali on my own, but she's heading to some kind of fandom con for her favorite show. She doesn't love traveling alone, so we decided to head out at the same time. She'll come home before me, but I'm happy to fly with her when I can.

Bernie is a pretty close friend, she's on my team, and she's a fucking kick-ass gamer. She's also funny and chill, and if she wasn't my teammate, I probably would have tried to hook up with her at some point.

Years ago—when we all formed Team NoMad—Dex, Simon, Link, and I all agreed Bernie was off limits. When Link left the team and Chuck filled his spot, we communicated the same to him. Though, I'm pretty sure that to this day, he's still scared of her. She would probably blow a gasket if she found out about our rule. But it was necessary and one of the reasons our team has flourished is because we don't have drama.

I find the playlist I'm looking for and settle in for the flight.

Several songs in, I feel a light tap on my shoulder. Arching a brow, I look at Bernie. She nods to my phone and I pause my music.

"At the risk of sounding all romantic, you should find her while you're in the city this week," Bernie says before popping some mini pretzels into her mouth.

I grunt and pull an earbud out of my ear. "That's random."

"I've been thinking about your surfer girl. I think you need to find her."

I shift toward her. "Why are you thinking about her? And how do you purpose I find her? Culver City isn't small."

Bernie smiles sweetly, and I can tell I'm in for one heck of an explanation.

"I've been thinking about her because I know you really like her." I open my mouth to ask her how she would know that, but she waves me off and continues. "All the times we've talked about her, I could tell you're bummed things didn't work out."

"Yeah, I'm still not one hundred percent sure how you found out about Kelly," I mutter. For real, though, about a week after I got home from my last trip to Lasso, she cornered me after an hours-long practice session and told me how sorry she was I lost "surfer girl's" number. My eyes nearly budged out of my head.

She tried to get me to talk about the whole ordeal. Because I guess meeting a girl at random multiple times over several months and not getting her number is considered an ordeal.

Needless to say, while back in Chicago over the past month, I've gotten the heavy reminder from both Garland and Bernie that I indeed fucked up with Kelly. Truth be told, I don't need their pesky reminders. I've got Kelly on my mind a lot and it's becoming an issue.

"Well, you know I'm friends with Garland, right?" She looks slightly annoyed.

"Garland has a big mouth," I rant, remembering that he and Bernie are friends. However, I didn't know they were good enough friends to gossip about me and my surfer girl.

"That he does. But I'm glad he told me about surfer girl. And, actually, to answer your other question, I have an idea on how to find her."

"Surfer girl has a name." I glare and her smile grows.

"See, you're into her. You want me to call her Kelly, which I will since you asked so politely."

I shake my head. *What the fuck?*

"Okay, Bern, let's get this over with. How do you suppose I find Kelly?"

"You need to return to the scene of the crime." Her

eyes wide and shoulders puffed, she seems to truly feel like she has the best idea. But I'm not sure I follow.

Narrowing my eyes, I ask, "Crime?"

"Go back to the places you saw her and try to find her again."

"I saw her at a coffee house, club, and the beach," I deadpan.

"The beach would probably make the most sense to return to. As you know, she's a surfer girl." She cocks her head like this should have been obvious.

"I'm not going to be able to get to the beach this trip. I'm flying out on the red-eye Friday night." I twist my lips, realizing she was on to something. But my flight can't be changed at this point without serious fees.

Bernie hums and pulls her bottom lip into her mouth while she thinks. "The coffee house then. Every morning before you head into Lasso, go there. And make sure it's the same time you saw her the first time. You do it every day until you find her."

I volley the idea around in my head. It's not bad. Maybe a little desperate. But fuck me if I'm not a little desperate to find her.

"That would probably work." I lift a shoulder, still thinking it through.

"It will work and when you see her again, Ben, put her fucking number in your phone before she walks away." She sighs and I roll my eyes.

"Shut it. I know already," I growl and she laughs.

"Carry on, Grouchy." She waves to my phone as she jumps right back into the book she's reading.

I do as she says, slightly annoyed we just had this whole conversation.

As we near the end of our flight, I feel a renewed sense of energy for this trip. I'm going to stalk the shit out of The Melting Moon for the surfer girl who got away.

PULLING my cup of coffee off the counter, I slowly walk through the café. I casually dart my gaze through the space, but I haven't yet seen the brunette beauty. Not while I was waiting to order or while in line for my drink. I make my way to a table next to the door and sit down, anxious at the fact that she hasn't shown. I peek at my watch and see it's the exact same time of morning as when I first set my eyes on her. I've only got about thirty minutes until I'm due at Lasso, and this is my last fucking chance. While I wasn't pumped about making camp here for the past three mornings, I did what I needed to do in order to find her. But damn if I don't hope she shows up in the next fifteen minutes.

Taking a sip of my coffee, I pull out my phone as a text vibrates its alert.

BURNDIT: Did she show?
Me: Not yet.
BurndIt: Patience, young padawan. She will show. I just know it.
Me: <Andy Samberg yeah right GIF>

I POCKET MY PHONE, not wanting to miss her if she comes through. But with every person who walks into Melting Moon, I grow increasingly less sure of this plan. Minutes later, I take one last gaze of the café as I leave for Lasso.

This was a stupid plan.

Fate has clearly stepped in and denied me one final chance to connect with Kelly. Yesterday morning, I was able to stay a bit longer than I had on Wednesday. This morning, I arrived even earlier. And she didn't show. Maybe her coming to Melting Moon was just a one-off. I thought I remembered her saying at breakfast how much she loved the café. Surely, we would have crossed paths. I know Garland has even been watching for her, but he hasn't seen her either.

Fine, asshole universe. I've received your message loud and clear. I'm a fucking idiot and missed my chance. Time to move on.

I TAKE a deep breath of fresh city air as I step out of the Lasso building. It's nearly six, and it was a long fucking day of final edits on the game I was voicing for. I have another project coming up next month, but for now, it feels good to complete a project.

My flight takes off at eleven forty-five tonight, so I've got about four hours to burn. I have the hotel room booked through tomorrow morning, but I opted to fly home late tonight because—well, there isn't a reason for me to stay. I'll meet Garland for dinner later, but for now, I need caffeine. So, I start my short walk to Melting Moon one last time. I notice the hours on the glass pane next to the door; they'll be closing soon. I'm thankful I didn't miss out on the tall black coffee I so desperately need before my flight tonight. Damn, I'd be in a bad way if I had to cut caffeine out of my life.

As I pull open the door, a woman nearly crashes into me.

"Oh," she mutters. Her head is down, staring at her phone, and she has a clear coffee cup in hand.

"Excuse me," I say, my tone clipped. She's not paying attention to where she's going, and I'm not interested in wearing her coffee down my shirt.

She looks up just as her shoulder rams into the doorjamb and her cup jerks out of her hand.

Fuck me.

Her ice-cold Frappuccino splatters over my lower torso and the crotch of my jeans. It's cold as fuck, but the icy beverage doesn't matter as I stare into the eyes of a startled, unbelieving Kelly.

"Kelly," I mumble as my name falls from her lips. God damn, I want to kiss those lips.

"Oh my God, Ben. I'm so sorry." She pushes toward me, and I take a few steps back. As if she suddenly remembered something, she tells me to hold on as she turns and nearly bumps into another patron who's trying to leave. I'm still in shock from coming face to face with her, and I just stand there, holding the door open. She walks back toward me with a wad of napkins in her hands. She places her hand on my chest, nudging me back out of the café. I let her do what she wants with me and take several steps back as she wipes at my lower abdomen, profusely apologizing.

"I'm so sorry, Ben. I wasn't watching where I was going," she mutters, worry laced in her tone.

I don't say anything as I stand there watching her attack what's left of the frap on my shirt. When her busy hands brush at the hem of my shirt, it jerks me out of my shock. I grab both arms, effectively stilling her, and she looks up at me. Worry, surprise, and something else cloud her eyes.

"Kelly," is all I can manage before I'm pulling her into me and kissing her.

The minute my lips touch hers, she stiffens, but I don't give her time to think. Brushing my lips over hers again, I press in harder. Angling my jaw, I swipe my tongue across her closed lips. I can't help the growl that rumbles in the back of my throat. It must jar her from her own shock, for her lips open, encouraging me to take more. She tastes of chocolate and coffee, and a fire ignites from deep within. I run my hand up her arm, over her shoulder, and wrap it around the nape of her neck, pulling her into me.

The chemistry between us is painfully strong, but this kiss—this kiss is damn near combustible. I catch her small moan with my lips and feel her desire all the way in my bones.

The bell of the café dings as the door opens, and I remember where we're standing. Out in public, in the middle of a crowded sidewalk. Regretfully, I break the kiss. Her eyes are still closed, and her face slightly flushed. Both of us are struggling for air.

"Kelly." I smirk, taking in her downright lustful state.

She blinks her eyes open, and they're heated from our kiss. "Are you trying to make sure you don't forget my name?"

I chortle. "No, why would you think that?" I lean slightly away from her, my hands still on her. That's when I realize there may still be heat in her eyes, but she isn't happy.

"You keep saying my name. I assume it's because you forgot who I was." She takes a step away from me and my arms drop, the last of our connection severed. The electricity between us fizzles out as if the power was cut.

"I'd never forget who you are," I tell her truthfully, then continue. "I just can't believe you're standing right here in front of me." I take her in. She's wearing a pair of jean shorts, a simple black T-shirt and black chucks. This look has got to be Kelly—her normal state of dress. And I can't lie, my dick twitches at the sight.

She looks to the sky and mutters something under her breath, but I only catch the word *fate*. When she zeros those green eyes back on me, she looks downright pissed. Gone is the lust-filled haze of our hot as fuck first kiss. And in its place is stone-cold anger.

"Well, it seems as though you forgot my number." It's not a question. It's not an accusation, either. It's a fact, and one she's clearly pissed about.

I lift my hands to try to calm her. "Kelly, I'm so sorry. It's a sad, sad story. One that I'm legitimately embarrassed to share, but you have no idea how glad I am to find you." I try not to beg, but I can tell by her stance that she may bolt and not give me a chance to explain. "I've been looking for you."

Her eyes narrow. "You have two minutes to explain."

I suck in a breath, knowing I have to make the next words out of my mouth count. "This is going to sound crazy, but the minute you left the diner, Garland spilled his drink and it took out your number within seconds. I couldn't believe my fucking luck. I just got back into town Wednesday, but every day this week, I've come here looking for you. Hell, even Garland has had his eyes peeled for you when he comes by for coffee."

I don't want to overwhelm her, so I leave my explanation at that. She studies me then says, "So you actually lost my number?" Her gaze is assessing, and I'm not sure where I stand with her right now.

"God's honest truth. I'm so fucking sorry, Kelly. I thought I was never going to see you again." I reach out and snag her hand. She lets me hold it, but she cocks a perfectly sculpted eyebrow at me. "Not getting your number at the club, then losing it at the diner, has had me in the shittiest mood for weeks now. I've been such a grouch that both Garland and my teammate Bernie have been urging me to stalk this place in hopes of finding you."

"And now you've found me, and my drink is all over your crotch." She waves toward my wet body, pulling her hand free at the same time. It's not until she reminds me that I remember I am, in fact, drenched.

"I don't even care," I declare.

"Come on, this place is about to close. I need a new frap." She turns, looking over her shoulder at me, and I follow like a dutiful puppy. She hasn't forgiven me, but she isn't running or pushing me away, so I follow and hope for the best.

We stand in silence as we order and wait for our drinks. When I offer to pay for hers, she protests, but I don't listen and whip out a twenty.

We can't stay in the café as it's closing up, so we head out the door, and she steers me to a nearby bench.

"Thanks for the drink," she says, pulling the straw between her lips.

"Thanks for hearing me out," I tell her.

"Honestly, I'd given up on hearing from you," she scolds. She glances at me but doesn't make eye contact.

"I'm really sorry, Kelly." I reach for her hand and squeeze it. The need to touch her, no matter how insignificant is nearly unbearable.

"You've really been looking for me?" She looks down at my hand covering hers.

"Yes. Grade-A stalking, sweetheart. Three full days." I chuckle.

She purses her lips. "And yet, you didn't actually find me. I took you by surprise."

"You've taken me by surprise since day one, so I expect nothing less." I smirk at her and see a flash of laughter in her face, but she shuts it down tight.

"Fair enough." She shrugs a shoulder.

I intertwine my fingers with hers and let out an easy breath when she doesn't push me away.

She heaves a heavy sigh and slowly turns her gaze to me. "I have a confession. I looked you up. Well, my friend Aubrey did. And we found you."

"But you didn't reach out," I surmise and feel a pang of regret. Maybe I did ruin this with all my stupidity.

"I wanted to. I almost did. I had an email written up and ready to send to your manager. But then I deleted it. For one, I didn't like having to go through someone else to reach you. And two, I was mad at you."

I clench my jaw, not liking her reasons but understanding them. She continues. "The last thing I wanted to do was reach out to a guy I thought was into me, but clearly, not enough to call. I understand now that's not the case, but that's where my head was at."

I nod my understanding but decide to direct the conversation to the present. Grinning, I scoot in a little closer to her, her bare thigh and my semi-soaked one brushing together. "Damn, I'm happy you ran into me. I honestly thought I was going to head back to Chicago without seeing you again."

Her face softens and I know I'm forgiven. At least for now.

"It's sweet that you came here so much." She bites on her lip. "But I don't live in the city anymore. I moved to Hermosa Beach two weeks ago."

Not letting the news deter me, I smile. I may not know her well yet, but I know the beach suits her. "I bet you're loving all the surfing."

She graces me with that beautiful smile. "It's amazing. I missed living on the beach."

"Was that why you moved?" I ask, before taking a drink of my piping hot coffee.

"A job opportunity, actually. My friend Aubrey runs an animal shelter in Hermosa and her manager is on maternity leave for a few months, so Aubrey asked me to cover for her. Normally, I would have passed—it's not a long-term job—but to be honest, I needed a change. I couldn't stand my old job, and the move had the added benefits of being near the beach and next door to my best friend. It felt like the right choice."

"That's awesome. I think it fits you perfectly. I'm happy for you, Kelly."

She narrows her eyes and then acquiesces and says, "Thank you."

"Funny how the universe steps in, yeah?" I lean back on the bench and watch the passersby hustle down the sidewalks, the traffic hitting rush hour as the streets start to become congested. I'm not looking at her, but I can see her head tilt to the side.

"How so?" she says, her voice full of question.

"We ran into each other four times. I live across the country, and you moved out of the city. We shouldn't have run into each other at all, but we did. I came here every day for the last three days, wondering if you would show up. And suddenly, on my way out of town, you just magically appear. The universe clearly stepped in. It's fate that we're sharing this bench right now." I smirk, lean in, and bump her shoulder.

"I don't know about fate. More like pure stupidity... on both our parts. You didn't get my number, then lost it when you had it. I doused you with a fresh cup of Frappuccino." She eyes my crotch area, her cheeks tingeing pink before dragging her focus back to me. I wink. "How are you dealing with the wet clothes right now?" she adds.

"It's uncomfortable as fuck, but this conversation is more important. I don't want to lose you again." Shit, I'm laying it on thick, but I think it's working.

The side of her lips tips up. "You're a sweet talker."

"Sure." I chuckle. We stare at each other for a minute, and just as I consider leaning over and kissing her again, she speaks.

"You kissed me." Her voice is heavy but low, and I know it's guided by lust.

"I did. And you kissed me back." I know my answering smile is affecting her when her eyes flutter to my lips.

"Hmm," she answers, and then just when I lean in, the moment is over when a flurry of honks and yells come from the nearby intersection. Her trance on my lips is broken when she looks away at the jumble of cars.

"You said you're heading home. Now? Tonight?" She doesn't look at me when she asks.

A feeling of dread overcomes me, and I fight through the disappointment. Of course, the universe would give us only a couple of hours. "Red-eye tonight. Have dinner with me." I reach out, cup her cheek, and gently angle her face back toward me. "Please," I whisper.

"Okay." She doesn't hesitate.

"Okay." I smile, my heart ramming into my chest.

"You should probably change, though." She glances down and then giggles. "You probably think I'm a hot mess."

I love that she can laugh at herself. That she isn't tearing herself down out of embarrassment. "Not at all. I find your clumsiness utterly adorable," I tell her truthfully.

She laughs and rolls her eyes. I lean in and kiss her, stealing the last of her giggles. I want to deepen the kiss, but I don't want to be interrupted when I do. We're still sitting on this uncomfortable bench.

Breaking the kiss, I pull away—but not very far. "Come back to my hotel with me so I can change. Then we'll go to dinner somewhere."

Her lips curve into a smile. "Okay."

Grudgingly, I pull away and stand. I pull my phone out of my pocket, and fortunately, it missed out on the Frappuccino. "Give me your number." My voice is thick and gravelly from the kiss. "Please," I add with a smile.

"I'm going with you. Do you really need it now?" Her voice is silky smooth.

I raise an eyebrow. "Babe, with our luck, a stampede of elephants is going to turn the corner there," I nod to the side street up ahead, "and we will have to make a run for it. We'll ultimately get separated, and I'll have to spend the rest of my life wondering if you survived or not."

Her head tilts back and her laugh nearly undoes me. "Oh my God, that's some imagination you've got there, Casanova." Once she gets her sexy self under control, she gives me her number and it's finally in my phone. As we walk toward my hotel, I text her to ensure she has my number as well. I'm not going to make the same fucking mistake—a what, third time?—and lose this girl. She's mine now.

EIGHT

Kelly

The short walk to Ben's hotel doesn't give me a whole lot of time to think through the past thirty minutes. The only thing my mind is hung up on is the scorching hot kiss in front of Melting Moon. My body burns as I relive the feel of his lips, his tongue devouring mine, and the way he grabbed ahold of me and didn't want to let go. He must be in tune with my thoughts because his hand squeezes mine, and when I look at him, his sexy smirk tells me he knows exactly what I'm thinking.

As we walk through the hotel lobby, I start to pull my hand out of his, causing him to slow his pace.

"I'll wait down here," I whisper. I'm suddenly scared to be alone with him in his hotel room.

"I don't think so. I'm not chancing you disappearing on me." He tugs my hand toward the elevator, and I continue to follow him anyway.

He looks over his shoulder at me, and with a smug grin, he adds, "Don't worry, it will be a quick change. I'll keep my hands to myself." The elevator magically slides open as we approach.

I giggle a little when he wiggles his brows at me and pulls me into the elevator. Truth is, I don't want him to keep his hands to himself. I want those strong, skilled hands all over my body. I also know he's pretty much a stranger, and I didn't make it twenty-six years in this life not understanding stranger danger. But Ben—and whatever's between us—is different. It's real and it's strong.

We stand side by side in the elevator, fingers still twined together as we ascend to the tenth floor. Moments later, he's pocketing his key card as we walk through his hotel room door. The lights are off but the blinds are open, and the early evening sun fills the room. The smell I'm starting to associate with Ben consumes my senses. His scent is a mix of mint and lemon. The room is tidy, the bed is made, and his suitcase is closed and sitting by the dresser. It's obvious he's packed and ready to go. It hits me hard as I realize how close we were to missing each other.

"Have a seat. I'll change quickly." He lifts his bag effortlessly to the end of the bed and unzips it.

"This is a nice room," I say, taking in the suite-like space. There's a big red couch near the door with a coffee table in front. It faces the big screen TV hanging on the wall above a sleek black dresser that holds a coffee maker and a bowl of snacks. The king bed looks so comfy, I can't help myself when I plop down on it, bouncing a bit.

Ben smirks but pulls out a pair of jeans. "Yeah, I like it. I get this room every time I'm in town."

"Really?" Surprise laces my question.

He chuckles. "Yeah, it's not a big deal. I guess I'm a creature of habit. I worked with a guy once while writing a strategy guide who always had to stay in a corner room on the seventh floor. It was… odd."

"Wow, that's crazy." I look around the room once more as he moves toward the bathroom. "You should leave something behind. Like, leave something in the bedside drawer and see if it's still here next time you come." I suck my lip into my mouth, realizing I don't know when I'll see him again.

"Like a note? See if anyone writes back?" He laughs but points to the nightstand. "There's a notepad and pen in there, write something while I change."

He disappears into the bathroom, closing the door but not latching it. I pull out said paper and pen and stare down at the paper, unsure of what to write.

"So if you're not living in Culver anymore, why are you here now?" he asks, his voice raised so I can hear him through the door.

"I'm having breakfast with my cousin and aunt for my aunt's birthday tomorrow. It was just easier to come tonight," I tell him, pressing the pen to the paper but not writing.

"And you just happened to stop for coffee?" he asks.

"Melting Moon is my favorite part of Culver City. It's been two weeks since my last hit. I missed it." I chuckle, but when I look up, he's walking out of the bathroom. He's changed out of his drenched clothes into a new pair of jeans, but he's sans shirt. I snap my mouth closed as I realize it was hanging open while I take in his tanned, hard abs covered in tattoos. I knew he had art on his arms, but I wasn't expecting a peppering of work on his abs and chest. One of the tats on his shoulder wraps around and covers a small portion of the back of his neck. There's so much ink, I can't focus on just one, and my eyes dart from piece to piece.

"Sorry, I forgot a shirt." He reaches up and runs his hand through his messy hair as he walks back to his suitcase.

"It's fine," I squeak. His eyes draw to mine and his

smile is bashful. He places his dirty clothes inside a drawstring bag and puts it into the suitcase before reaching in and pulling out a shirt.

He lets out a low moan. "You keep looking at me like that, I'm not going to be able to keep my promise."

"What promise?" My voice comes out breathy, and I feel the need to fan myself. His answering chuckle causes a thousand little dragonflies to ignite in my belly. I drag my gaze up his hairless, sculpted chest, to his chin and full lips. They're quirked in a half-grin to his blazing hot eyes.

"To keep my hands to myself," he says as he—oh, so very slowly—tugs his shirt over his head. He smooths his hand down the front of his shirt, his hand sliding to the waistband of his jeans. I imagine him popping open the button, deciding that dinner is overrated, and I have to catch a whimper before I let it slip out. I'm still laser-focused on his hand as he pats his back pocket.

"Ah, my wallet," he says and walks back to the bathroom. That's when the pen, still pressed to the paper, starts to write on its own accord. Looking down at my message, I can't help but bite my lip.

I want to spend hours tracing all that ink with my tongue.

SENDING a quick thought to the universe that this doesn't backfire on me, I smile to myself, fold the note, then slide it to the back of the drawer. Just as I close the drawer, he comes back out.

"If we don't leave for dinner right now, Kelly, I can't promise you'll get fed." His gravelly voice catches me off guard. "Well, with food, that is." A painful sounding chuckle follows.

I slowly push off his bed and walk toward him. "It's okay. Let's go eat. It will make coming back here all that more rewarding."

"Fuck me," he mutters as I grab his hand and yank him toward the door.

"Promise?" I peek over my shoulder and wink at him. *I've got game too, folks.*

We walk to dinner, making idle chit-chat as we go. We don't get far from his hotel when his hand brushes mine and our fingers interlock without thought. Once seated, I waste no time getting to know him more.

"So, tell me more about your job." I lean my chin on my palm and smile.

"Which one?" He smirks and takes a drink of water. We sit at the four-top table in the middle of the busy dining room. But instead of sitting on the opposite side of the table, he casually sat next to me.

Tapping my finger to my lips, I decide. "The voice-over gig."

He launches into what he's doing at Lasso, and I must admit, the whole video game creation is intriguing. You ever have a moment when someone's telling you about their job and your eyes glaze over because it's so boring? Well, that's not Ben's job. Not at all.

"I'll be honest, I've never been into video games. I play a mean Candy Crush, but video games were never part of my life. But your job sounds fascinating. Both of them." I rest my hand next to my plate, and he extends his pinky and brushes it against mine.

"Candy Crush is solid." He chuckles.

"Can you be friends with a non-gamer?" I giggle.

"Yeah, I think I'll manage. You seem worth it." His

smirk is sexy, and I want to kiss it off his face right here and now. But just then, the server stops by and refills our glasses. Ben's foot finds mine under the table. His thick calf plants itself between my legs, effectively tangling us together. It's not an overly sexual move, but we are touching and it seems as if the urge to touch each other is getting stronger and stronger.

"You mentioned at the diner that you haven't been doing the game narrating for long." I want to ask if this is something he'll continue to do, but I don't want to sound needy. He nods and chimes in before I can ask.

"Yeah, I guess I just feel like change is near, so I wanted to branch out a bit. I can't be a professional gamer forever. I'll need a fallback." His finger lightly traces circles on my upturned hand that sits between us.

"Sounds sensible." My voice is breathy and unsteady. "Do you think narrating video games is your next step?"

He smiles down at our hands, "Nah, but I think it's a foot in the door." He looks up at me. "Lasso is a company I'd love to work for when my gaming days are behind me."

"Ah, sounds like you've got it figured out." I tip my head to the side, smiling, and he winks. My heart pounds in my chest, and I twist my lips to hide another grin. His flirt game is strong and I'm loving it. This is one of the most enjoyable dinners I've been on in a long time.

"Do you have things figured out?" he asks, just as our food is placed in front of us. I sit back, severing our connection by moving my hand off the table. As soon as we're alone again and start to dig into our food, he asks again.

"Uh, that would be a negative." I chuckle, cutting into my barbecue chicken breast. "I just haven't found my calling yet."

"That's all right. You're only, what…" his face

scrunches and I realize he's trying to guess my age. I laugh and offer him the answer. "See, you're only twenty-eight. You've still got time."

"Well, thank you for the confidence boost, but I'd like to figure it out sooner than later." I take a bite of chicken.

"What doesn't work for you?" He eats his own food, and I have to admit that his steak looks just as amazing as my chicken.

"I know I don't like corporate America, and I'm not sure I love office work," I tell him honestly.

"Meh, office work is overrated. I bet you're loving the animal shelter then."

I nod because he's spot-on. "I'm really enjoying it. My degree is in general business, but I got a minor in management. I'm loving running the shelter from day-to-day."

"I'm sure the furry co-workers you spend your day with help." He shrugs.

I lean back in my chair and laugh. "You have no idea how hard it is to not take my work home with me."

"I can almost guarantee you'll adopt a four-legged friend by the time I'm back in Cali." He chuckles. While I don't doubt him, this does give me the perfect opening.

"And when will that be?" I go for nonchalant, and I think I pull it off when he answers without hesitation.

"Three weeks. I'll be back for four days, then gone a week and back for another four days."

He must read the concern on my face. I can feel that my face is all scrunched. "What's wrong?" he asks.

"How do you handle all the travel? Wouldn't it be easier to stay longer and get it all done in one go?" I look up at him, resting my fork on the plate.

"Well, there are several months each year where I'm traveling a lot. And I have to fit the narrating into my schedule. Lasso is great about it. They mostly want my voice because I'm on a championship gaming team, so they make it work." His tone is noncommittal, like all that travel isn't a big deal. "I've got a shit-ton of frequent flyer miles racked up. It's ridiculous."

"I don't think I could handle all the traveling." I twist my lips and think about that kind of life.

"I'm used to it. I have no reason to be home for weekends or throughout the week, really. My work is my life right now."

We finish our meal while I tell him about Aubrey and Chance, and he tells me about his teammates. When we're asked about dessert, he glances at his watch, and when he looks up at me, there's pure heat in his eyes.

"Your choice, Kelly. I've got about ninety minutes until I've got to head to LAX."

I know what I want for dessert. While I've lost some of my confidence and am unable to make a sexy reply, I ask for the check without looking at the server. Ben's smile grows, and he leans in while I do the same.

His hot breath at my ear, he says, "Good choice." And then he lightly kisses the soft spot right under my ear. A shiver zings through my body, and I hear his soft chuckle as he does it again.

I fight back a moan just as a throat is cleared, and the server sets down the check. Ben pulls away and tugs his wallet out of his back pocket.

I don't even remember him signing the receipt or exiting the restaurant. Rushing through the busy sidewalks back to his hotel is all a blur. We share heated smiles and intertwined fingers as we ride the elevator. Suddenly, my mind seems to float back into the here and now as he grips my hand tighter and pulls me down the hall to his room.

A burning sensation of anticipation fills my chest as we nearly stumble into his room. He pulls his wallet and phone from his pockets, depositing them and his key card on the side table. I walk to the bed, plopping down in the spot I sat earlier.

We stare at each other as the lights from the city twinkle into the room, but his face is slightly shadowed. He leans over and snaps on the table lamp. It doesn't add much light, but there's enough for me to take him in with a deep sigh.

He moves a step closer to me and then another, the sound of his footsteps cutting through the silence of the room. Blood rushes to my ears, and my hands tingle to reach out to him.

In a swirl of motion, he's in front of me, our knees touching. I spread mine, and he doesn't hesitate to step between my legs. Looking up at his handsome face, all I see is heat and desire.

He leans down and catches my lips. Fire sears through me as he brushes his lips over mine. Urging my lips apart, his tongue sweeps into my mouth, shifting the kiss from persuasive to demanding. A soft moan from the back of my throat causes us both to lose control. Grabbing a fistful of his soft shirt, I pull him down to me as I lean back on the bed. Bracing himself over me, I slide my hands under his shirt.

After that, the race to rid ourselves of our clothes is on. His shirt comes off, mine goes flying. His pants and my shorts collect in piles near the bed. He wastes no time freeing me of my bra and undies. And I don't give him a chance to explore before I push his boxers down his hips.

The pleasure on his face as I gently wrap my hand around him results in a low hiss. I smirk at the reaction, and he leans down and nips my earlobe, sending a shiver of desire down my spine. This push and pull between us—this teasing—continues. Our kissing deepens as his hands roam over me, my hands gliding over his hard, lickable body as if I can't decide on a place to land.

"I need you," I say on a raspy moan.

"Yeah," he moans, but he leans away from me, reaching for the bag still at the end of the bed. He unzips an outside pocket and digs around, seconds later, producing a condom. With heavy anticipation I watch him as he covers himself and then nestles himself right at my core. His cocky smile and heated stare cause me to smile as I reach up and cup his cheek.

"I need you. Now, Ben," I demand, and suddenly, I can't breathe as I feel the hard thickness of him slide inside me. Then I gasp for air as he starts moving his hips, my own movements matching his pattern. We move together, breathing in deep gasps of each other's air. Hands roaming, grabbing, pulling. Lips smashing, tasting, nipping. Moans and grunts that are probably more animalistic than sexy fill the hotel room.

He reaches a hand between us, slowly circling where I need him most. My fingers twist deep into his hair only an instant before I cry out in pure bliss. A searing bolt of pleasure strikes through me. Ben stares down at me, his eyes full of molten heat as they watch me fall apart. Before I'm able to catch my breath and come back to earth, he leans down and catches the last of my gasps with his lips, finding his own release in the process.

He falls onto me, burying his face in the nape of my neck. I draw my arms around him and drag my fingers softly down his back. He places a gentle kiss on my neck in response as he adjusts, and the loss of him brings a coldness I wasn't expecting. He returns to me a beat later and gathers me in his arms. Unfamiliar tenderness sweeps through me as we lay in a heap of bones and limbs in his bed. Well, his hotel bed.

I've never had such an earth-shattering orgasm before. Even with past boyfriends, the need to linger, to lay completely open and be one hundred percent me, has never consumed me before. The tightness in my chest starts to ache as the realization that he's about to leave works its way through my thoughts. It is too soon for love, that's for sure. I barely know Ben, but it isn't too soon for all-consuming lust, and I can tell if given the chance, falling in love with him isn't far off.

Biting my lip, I will my heart to stop racing.

"That... That was..." His voice is still husky with sex.

"Amazing?" I offered.

"Yeah," he says around a sigh.

We lie there for a few more moments, catching our breaths. Is he thinking about what's next for us? He's leaving. He has no choice—his home isn't here. What could we possibly become to one another? As if he can hear my thoughts, he breaks the silence once more.

"I have to leave soon." His voice is steady, but there's a wariness with how he says it.

"I know," I breathe out unhappily, and there's silence once more. After several beats, I ask the obvious. "What happens now?"

His arm tightens around me as he lets out a deep, jagged sigh. "I can't do long distance." His tone is pained as his words hit my ears. I hadn't thought about a long-distance relationship, only that there would be distance between us.

"All right," I whisper.

We both continue staring up at the popcorn-speckled ceiling. It's as if we both understand this conversation is easier to have in this way. We're still completely naked, tangled in each other's arms, yet without eye contact.

"I want to be something to you." His voice startles me.

"I don't want to just be that guy you ran into several times and slept with that one time. I don't want to lose you." His words burn in my veins. He feels this pull between us. It's bigger than we both expected, and it's not worth letting go of... yet.

On a shaky breath, I offer the option most don't want to hear. "Friends, then?" His chuckle vibrates through my body. "There aren't many other options, Ben."

He sighs. "I know, Kel." The nickname results in tiny tingles in my toes, belly, and chest. "I'm not sure what this says about me. It probably means I'm a selfish asshole. But I want to do this again. I don't think I'll be able to forget everything that just happened between us. I'm not done experiencing you yet."

I suck in a gasp. The reality of his words hits me hard, and I'm momentarily at a loss of how to answer him.

"See. I'm an asshole," he mutters. He starts to roll away, but I push up to my elbow, yanking his arm and halting his attempt to leave the bed. Finally, we brave each other's stare.

"If you are, then I am." His lips press together, his eyes blaze with amusement.

"You're not an asshole," he tells me.

"I'm not done with you, either. I just found you. So if you can't do long distance, then friends it is. But with benefits." I don't register the deal I'm offering as anything other than desperation to keep him in my life. I won't think about how offering all of myself to someone every few weeks, for just sex, will slowly tick away at my heart. I know the more time I spend with him, the more I'll fall. My heart is too soft. It's not strong enough to withstand this kind of disaster waiting to happen. But I don't care. I need Ben in my life. So I'll take what I can get.

He narrows his eyes, all traces of humor gone. "Kelly, is that what you want?"

"Yes," is all I allow myself to say.

He stares down at me, seeming to process my offer. It's a stellar offer—one most guys would snag up in a heartbeat. But Ben weighs my words, thinking them through with careful consideration. And my heart shifts just a millimeter in my chest. He's a good man.

His eyes glance at my lips, then he focuses his gaze back on my eyes. If this wasn't such an important moment, I'd commend him for not looking further. He clears his throat. "If you're sure, then I'll take it."

"I'm sure," I tell him.

I'm sure my heart will fall completely and utterly in love with you.

His smile is devilish. He leans in to kiss me, but music from his phone interrupts the moment.

"Shit," he mutters. He places a kiss on the tip of my nose. "That's my warning. I've got to get to the airport."

We both climb out of the bed, finding our clothes and quickly dressing. It's disorienting to think I've only been in his presence for a couple of hours, yet it feels like I've been with him for much longer. I fear saying goodbye to him is going to feel as if we'd been with each other for weeks. I reel myself in. I'm getting ahead of myself.

The room is silent. I wait for him by the door as he gathers his suitcase and slings a heavy-duty backpack over his shoulders. He doesn't grab my hand like I expect him to as we walk to the elevator.

Friends. Friends. Friends. I repeat the word in an attempt to trample down my disappointment.

We don't speak until we stand just outside the hotel. He turns to me with a smile that doesn't quite reach his eyes.

"This isn't goodbye, Kel. I'll be back in a few weeks. We'll see each other then, yeah?"

I force a smile and nod. "Yeah."

"I'll text you."

I narrow my eyes. "I've heard that one before."

He barks out a laugh, breaking the state of wariness between us. "I promise."

Laughter dances in his eyes. I take him in one last time. He's tall, dark, and handsome, his hair still messy from my fingers. His tatted-up arms are on display thanks to his simple black T-shirt. I'm still shocked at how much of a contradiction he is. His looks scream bad boy, but he's so nice and good. And a bit nerdy. He grunts as I draw my eyes back up to his face, his scruff nearly causing my mouth to water.

"Fuck, Kelly," he mummers and pulls me into him for a deep, wildly inappropriate kiss. Kissing him back, all logical thought slips away, and I forget we'd just decided to be friends. We'll see each other when he returns, but this isn't by any means, a romantic relationship. But I guess this friendship includes sexy as hell goodbye kisses.

He pulls away, his cocky grin in place while I remain breathless.

"Bye, Kel." He winks and hops into the waiting Uber.

Just like that, my new friend is gone. I stare after the black sedan for a moment too long and watch it turn the corner. Shaking myself out of the trance, I head to my old apartment.

This will work.

This will be fine.

Now I have something to look forward to next month.

I'll be fine.

I tell myself the same things over and over, even though I worry we'll fall into the same broken record we've become. He won't call and we won't see each other again. But, I remember I have his number now, and if we truly want to be friends, the communication goes both ways.

Yet not even an hour later, I get an unexpected text. One that has me grinning from ear to ear.

BEN: Just got to the airport and wanted to be sure to keep my promise. This is me, texting you. Miss you already, friend.

THE NEXT MORNING at brunch with my cousin and aunt, my phone vibrates in my pocket. I pull it out while my cousin talks about work and I can't contain the smile.

BEN: Made it home. Long flight. Thought of you the whole way home.
Me: Glad you're home.
Ben: Gonna catch some ZZZs before the team meeting this afternoon. Text ya later.
Me: Sweet dreams.
Ben: <winky face>

MY BODY RELAXES A BIT, basking in the realization that he's keeping his word. That this might work. Whatever *this* turns into.

NINE

Ben

I lean back into my pro-series gaming chair and huff out a sigh. I just spent the last two hours in a heated practice round for our upcoming tournament this weekend. We're going to kick ass, but that was intense. I scrub my hand down my face and close my eyes. On my desk, my phone pings, and I reach for it. As I swipe at the text, I can't help but smile.

KELLY: My surf suit. I'm <surfboard emoji>

I GROAN, remembering the one and only time I've seen her in her surf suit. It was hot as hell, and I wish I could see her in it again. This is the first I've heard from her today, but I do the math and realize she should probably be at work right now.

. . .

Cocky Gamer

ME: At ten in the morning on a Wednesday?

Kelly: Well, no. Right now, I'm wearing jeans and a shirt, but when you texted, I was indeed wearing my surf suit. I thought that would be more exciting.

Me: Ah, well, thanks for considering my feelings on the matter.

Me: You're looking sexy in that surf suit.

Kelly: <blush>

Kelly: What are you wearing?

Me: Nothing. <winky face>

I SMIRK because I'm not naked, but I want to see where this goes. We've been texting every day since my last trip. I know we decided on just being friends who have sex when I'm in Cali, but I'm horny as hell and can't wait to get her alone in a room again. So I've decided to push a little, see where it gets us.

KELLY: Isn't it like one p.m. in Chicago?

Me: Yeah, but I got hot.

Kelly: Really?

Me: Yup. I'm sitting at my desk and started thinking about that romp in my hotel room and got all hot and bothered.

Kelly: So you took off all your clothes?

Kelly: Did you say, 'It's getting hot in here' first?

Me: Smart-ass

Kelly: Is there a reason you're trying to bait me into thinking you're naked?

Me: Sigh

Me: I was curious how far we'd take it.

. . .

SHE'S smart and I'm honest. This would have probably been a better text for late tonight, but my timing with her has never been great.

I push away from my desk, twisting my chair to take a break from my screen.

KELLY: I commend your attempt. But as you know, it's not even lunch for me and I'm at work.

Kelly: Were you hoping the thought of you naked and thinking about our amazing sexual encounter was going to get me all hot and bothered? Causing me to go hide in the private restroom, lock the door behind me, and then ask you to touch yourself while I slowly and deliberately imagine it's your fingers touching my wet, hot center?

FUCKING HELL.

Suddenly the room is too hot. The picture she's painted of her touching herself to thoughts of me has my dick hard and me instantly regretting I didn't try this later tonight.

KELLY: Are you touching yourself right now?
Me: You're evil.
Kelly: You started it.
Me: I don't know what I was thinking.
Kelly: That you miss my body and can't wait for your visit next week?
Me: I miss more than just your body. But, yeah.
Kelly: I miss you, too.
Kelly: But I have to go now. Duty calls.

Me: All right.

Kelly: Call me tonight after eight my time. We can talk about you being naked and me touching myself.

Me: Shit, Kel. How am I gonna wait so long?

Me: But fine. I'll wait. Have a good rest of your day.

Kelly: Talk to you later, gamer.

I LET OUT a breath and dig my head into the back of my chair, closing my eyes. Visions of her naked and touching herself fill my head. Calling her after eight her time means calling her after eleven here. I'm a night owl, so it doesn't matter too much. But I need relief now. I twist my wrist and look at the time, noting I've got a few minutes before I need to meet with the team. I've got time to rub one out. Feeling like a fucking sixteen-year-old unable to handle my horniness, I duck into the bathroom.

Twenty minutes later, feeling very little relief and a hell of a lot of anticipation for tonight, I walk into the team's training room. Late, of course, but it's not a big deal.

"Nice of you to show up," Simon says from the overstuffed leather couch shoved against the wall of the living room.

Our training room is the size of two, two-bedroom apartments. The team—and by team, I mean our manager, Rob—bought this unit and the one next to it after our first year going pro. He worked out some kind of deal to have it remodeled to make it work for our training. The large, open living room holds a gaming station for each of us. Desks, high-powered PCU's, and gaming systems at each. We have two monitors apiece and big, expensive, comfortable gaming chairs. A lot of the extra bells and whistles that deck out our stations are courtesy of sponsors and potential sponsors. As a team, we have several, but Dex, Simon, and Bernie have a lot of individual sponsors as well. Chuck doesn't like the spotlight, and I've had a few over the years but find it annoying to commit to specific products. I won't turn away free products that the others get and generously share with the team, though.

The training unit also has a stocked kitchen and dining area, two bathrooms, a bedroom, and a workout room. The bedroom isn't used, as we all have our own places, but it's there in case it's needed. The workout room is the equivalent of a small gym and gets used quite a lot by Dex, Simon, and myself. I've never seen Bernie step foot in it, and Chuck really isn't the fitness type.

We all live in this same apartment building, which is handy. Chuck and I room together down the hall, and Bernie has her own unit on the same floor as well. On the floor directly above us, Simon and Link share a three-bedroom, as Dex just moved out to live with his girlfriend or fiancée—I'm not sure what she is. He and Morgan didn't go far, though; only to the floor directly below. Honestly, Dex might own this building. He's fucking loaded. He's made bank on sponsors and winnings, and he turns around and invests smartly. Yeah, I wouldn't be surprised if he owns the building, but I don't ask because it's none of my business how he spends his money.

"Sorry," I groan.

"It's okay, Ben. We waited." Bernie smiles as she comes out of the kitchen with a can of pop.

We need to talk about our upcoming tournament and practice schedule for the next few weeks. While we do, Bernie writes on the giant hanging wall calendar and adds events to our digital group calendar. She's a kick-ass gamer, but honestly, we would be lost without her organization skills, too. Most of the time, I think she manages our time better than our actual manager. I'm nearly positive he relaxes a bit because he knows she's got us. Lord help him when she retires.

I wonder what she's going to do when she doesn't game professionally anymore. I look around at each member of my team and think about our lives after gaming. Dex will probably end up owning and running some gaming company. Simon will probably do coding or design work. Bern, well, she'll need to manage something important. And Chuck—hell, I don't even know. And me? I need to figure my shit out.

As Bernie wraps up the meeting, I'm pulled from my thoughts and remember I have something to add. "I'll be at Lasso next week, Tuesday through Friday. But I'll be staying an extra two days."

"Oh, gonna party it up in Cali?" Dex laughs, knowing it's not my scene.

"Yeah, sure." I chuckle.

"You staying to hang out with Kelly?" Bernie asks, her eyes wide and all dreamy and shit.

"Oh, yeah, Kelly. How's that going, man?" Simon punches my shoulder as he sits next to me on the couch.

"Good. She's good. And, yeah, I'm gonna stick around and hang out with her for a couple of days." I shrug, not wanting to make a big deal over it.

"I'm so excited for you and happy you two finally connected," Bern says, still with hearts in her eyes. She's such a romantic.

"Are you two an item now?" Simon asks. Dex leans forward, his arms on his knees, apparently just as interested as Simon and Bernie.

"Just friends," I tell the room.

"Are you sure? You guys are always texting, and I thought for sure there was a ton of chemistry between the two of you." Bernie's face scrunches. Damn it, I'm not a huge fan of talking about my relationships.

"Did you meet her?" Dex asks, surprised.

Bernie looks to Dex. "No, but from what Garland has told me, their chemistry is through the roof."

Fucking Garland Thorpe.

"Garland should shut his mouth. Yes, we have chemistry. And the sex is phenomenal." Dex and Simon nod with understanding, and Bernie's eyes nearly pop out of her head. "But we're just friends."

"Why?" Simon leans back, giving me a look of challenge.

"Long distance, man. I can't do it. She wasn't into it, either." I cross my arms, not thrilled at how we ended up going down this road.

"Did she say that?" Bernie questions.

"She said staying friends was fine. But we… decided we'd add in benefits when I visited." I smirk, and Simon lifts his hand and high-fives me.

"So you two are just friends who have sex whenever you're in town," Dex confirms. I nod. Then he blows my mind out of the fucking water. "So what's stopping her from dating and hooking up with other dudes when you're not in town? Which is most of the time."

Fuck. Me.

"Oh snap," Simon chortles.

Bernie's eyes bug out and she quickly adds, "I doubt she's hooking up with other guys, Ben."

But Bernie doesn't know Kelly, so she's saying that solely for my benefit. I can't see Kelly being the kind of girl who sleeps with more than one guy. But, hell, we made it clear we're just friends.

"Maybe—and this is something you should talk to her about—but maybe you two should make whatever this is more than just a friendship. You don't have to call it a relationship if that makes you squeamish, but you could shoot for exclusive friends with benefits," Dex ponders.

"You two talk every day, Ben. I know you like her a lot, so don't shy away from having the tough conversations." Bernie's eyes dance with concern, her tone calm and thoughtful.

From his game station, Chuck so obliviously says, "Are we gonna practice or what, ladies?" He's never interested in personal shit. While I don't gossip like some of my teammates, Chuck would prefer to have zero personal connection with any of us. It makes living with the guy interesting, that's for sure.

Simon grumbles but stands, joining Dex as they head to their own desks.

Bernie leans down and pats my jean-clad knee. "Don't let her get away, Ben. Talk to her."

I push all thoughts of Kelly and our status out of my head and put all my focus into the several rounds we play of *Call of Battle*. But I won't lie—it's not far from my mind for the rest of the day.

I really like Kelly. If she were here in Chicago, or I was full time in Culver City, then hell yeah, I'd pursue more with her. But long-distance relationships suck ass. I've never been in one, but I know enough to know they would suck. So for now, she's just my friend, and I'm already having a hard time dealing with not getting to see her on the regular.

While she's amazing and I'm looking forward to seeing her again, I just don't think I can offer her any more than friendship. Maybe some sexting, phone sex, and a hookup when I'm in town.

She said she was down for friendship, and she seems down for phone sex, too. I just hope she's really okay with us keeping things this way. I guess time will tell.

Fuck. I'm just not sure if I'm ready for it to not be okay.

TEN

Kelly

I'm feverishly cleaning up my tiny apartment over the garage. I've picked up, dusted, cleaned the bathroom and kitchen, and now I've got just a bit of time left to do a quick vacuum. I'm a clean person, but I'll admit I do a horrid job of deep cleaning. If I had a surprise visitor, they wouldn't think my place is dirty—not at all. But if they looked closer, they'd see dust and dirt, I'm sure. I try to spend a few hours once a month deep cleaning. Sometimes it happens, sometimes it doesn't. But tonight, Ben is coming over.

And since this is the first time he's seen my place, I want it to be perfect. Not that it matters—we're just friends. But still. I'm too excited for him to be around this weekend. I was nearly shocked stupid when he told me last week he was going to extend his stay in Cali. He asked if I was busy over the weekend and if we could hang out. Of course, I have no plans, as I spend a lot of time staying in and reading or binge-watching TV. That's when Aubrey normally drags me out of the house.

I look up at the clock on the wall and see he should be

here soon. I rushed home after my shift at the shelter to shower and clean before he arrives. He was scheduled at Lasso until five, then planned on taking an Uber to Hermosa. The drive is about forty-five minutes, but I didn't know if he was going to check into his hotel first. Which was something I meant to talk to him about this week, but I chickened out. If he's coming to visit me, shouldn't he just stay with me? I don't know why I didn't offer it up, but I was worried he'd think it was too much of a girlfriend thing to offer.

While we've talked every day, and we've even participated in some super hot and fun phone sex, we still have this friendship vibe going. I know, I know, it's what we decided on—together.

Shutting off the vacuum, I start to roll up the cord when there's a knock at my front door. I take in a deep breath and go to open it up.

I'm disappointed when I don't find a sexy hot gamer at my door, but my best friend and her husband. Aubrey wears a massive smile on her face, and Chance casually leans against the railing that lines the tiny balcony outside my door.

"You look good, Kel. Even though you're clearly disappointed to see us." She smiles and takes in my black shorts and purple off the shoulder top. I was going for casual, yet sexy. Her delight and compliment tell me I've accomplished my goal.

"I'm not disappointed to see you. I just wasn't expecting you," I tell her and wave her in. But Aubrey shakes her head and takes a step back.

"We'll be quick." She bites her lip and my stomach drops. I drag my gaze to Chance, his hands in his pockets as he gives me a *I'm sorry* look.

"What did you do?" I whisper, not sure what to expect.

"Well, I did you a favor. A massive," her eyes widen and she drags out the word, "favor. I happen to know the booking manager at the hotel Ben is staying at while he's here."

"At the Holiday Inn?" I mumble.

"Yup. She and I go way back." Aubrey grins. I catch Chance's head shake that contradicts her words. My eyes narrow on her as she glances over her shoulder at her husband. Glaring, she huffs, "Okay, fine, we've known each other for a few months. But anyway, I consider her a friend, and I kinda, maybe, sorta, talked her into losing Ben's booking and telling him they didn't have any more vacancies." She fiddles with the bracelets on her wrist, and I can tell she's slightly nervous of my reaction.

"And how is this a favor exactly?"

"Now he has nowhere to stay, and you can offer up your place. See, just helping my girl out." Only for the first time since opening my door does she look even remotely unsure of herself.

"And you supported this deception?" I cut my eyes at Chance. He puts his hands up and waves them in front of him.

"I told her it was a risky move, but ultimately, I decided to stand by and let her do her thing." He shrugs like it's no big deal.

"Lies. You hesitated all of about two minutes before you got on the phone with the two other hotels and asked them to blacklist Ben Ford." Aubrey shoves her handsome, up-to-no-good husband in the shoulder. He chuckles, but she still has the common sense to look appalled.

My mouth drops open when I register what she said. "You did what, now?"

"Don't worry, I just asked them to blacklist him for the weekend." He gives a dismissive wave of his hand.

I stare at the two of them, and they stare back with big grins on their stupid, lovely faces.

"Oh my God, I hate you both." I let out a harsh breath and then pivot back into my apartment, leaving them standing outside. Pushing my hands into my hair and closing my eyes, I consider what they did. Ben's going to be mad.

"He's not," Aubrey says quietly, then I realize I said that last part out loud.

I twirl around on them and see they're both still outside. I shake my head, trying to get it on straight.

"Okay, okay. He doesn't have to know you two were up to no good. But you two—stop interfering." I point at them and give them my best *I mean it* face.

"Done." Aubrey's answering smile still worries me. I walk back to the door to send them on their way just as Ben hits the bottom step. The couple turns, and all three of us take him in.

My heart skips a beat, per usual when my eyes peruse his dark jeans, chucks, and dark blue shirt. It seems to be his normal look, but I can tell from the top of the steps that his shirt is butter soft, and what's underneath is rock hard. I fight back a whimper. It's been almost four weeks since I last saw him.

As my eyes travel up his chest and take in his slightly scruffy face, my eyes lock with his. He smirks and says, "Hey, Kel." His voice—deep, gravelly, and sexy—sends hundreds of tiny little bees through my body.

"Hey, Ben." My voice is breathier and wobblier than I expected. He continues up the steps, taking them two at a time—his long legs make it look natural. We don't break eye contact as he reaches the top of the landing. We're only a half-dozen steps apart, and my body tries to jerk forward as if to launch myself at his hard, taut body. But I refrain.

Still, I'm worried it's written all over my face. That's when I hear someone clear their throat.

The spell broken, I slide my gaze to my annoying neighbors. To hell with calling them my friends.

"Ben, this is Aubrey and her husband Chance. They live over there," nodding to the house to the left, "and were just leaving."

Aubrey gasps as she pretends to be offended. "Rude," she says to me, but I can see a glitter of laughter in her eyes. She turns back to Ben and holds out her hand. "Aubrey Bateman. It's so nice to finally meet you. I've heard so much about you."

I roll my eyes. Ben is polite and takes her hand to shake it, then looks behind her and shakes Chance's hand as he introduces himself. Once pleasantries are over, I try to shoo my nosy neighbors away.

"All right, well, didn't you guys have somewhere to be?" I look down at my watch to pretend to note the time.

Aubrey's nose scrunches and her mouth opens to respond, but Chance interrupts. "Yes, we do. You guys enjoy your night. It was great meeting you, Ben." Aubrey huffs next to him as he smiles at us and turns her toward the steps. They start to descend the stairs, but she yells over her shoulder as they go.

"I'm making brunch tomorrow. You should come and eat with us so we can get to know you better, Ben." It's not a question, and I know my friend well enough that if we don't say yes right now, she'll pester me until we show up for the meal.

"Fine," I tell her. Ben stepped closer to my door in an effort to let them pass, so when I reach out and grab his hand, it's not a stretch. I yank him toward me and into the doorway.

"Come in before she comes back," I tell him.

He chuckles and steps into my apartment. He's so close that the scent of him fills my lungs. I still have hold of his hand as I close the door. I look up at him, and his smile nearly causes my knees to wobble.

"Hi." His tone is soft.

"Hi," I whisper back.

"I missed you."

My lips tip up. "I missed you, too."

His face turns pensive for a moment. "I ran into a minor issue before I arrived." I try not to show that I know exactly what he's about to say.

"And what's that?"

"Seems as if my hotel reservation was lost. I called the other two hotels in town and they're booked." My eyes widen at his words. "Is there some big event going on this weekend?"

"Not that I know of. That's crazy, though." I press my lips together. "You can just stay here." I tilt my head toward the space behind me.

His gaze darts around the room and stops as he peers down the hall. Undoubtedly knowing that's where my bed is. I'm not sure if he'll expect to stay in my bed or if he'll assume he'll be on the couch. I suppose we will see how the night goes.

"If you don't mind." He swallows. "It would allow us more time together, too." He reaches up and scratches the side of his cheek.

"Yeah, absolutely. I was actually going to offer it as an option, but you booked your hotel room before I could." I shrug and walk further into my living room. He follows, leaving his suitcase by the front door. Shrugging off his backpack, he sets it on the floor by the couch.

"Nice little place you've got here." He looks around the space again.

I snort. "It's tiny. I'm lucky it has an actual bedroom and isn't just all open-concept. But it's my space for now, and I love it." I look around to see what he sees and spy my vacuum near the kitchen.

"I was cleaning when Aubrey and Chance stopped by. Let me get this." I rush over and wrap up the cord and then roll the vacuum to the very tiny hall closet. Shutting the door, I feel him at my back.

"Kelly," he growls.

I slowly turn, looking up at him. He's standing right in front of me.

My name is all he says as he leans down and claims my lips. Instantly, my arms fling around him, and I waste no time swiping my tongue into his wet, hot mouth. He moans then leans down and lifts me, my legs snaking around his hips.

Pressing myself into him, my fingers dig into his hair. He pushes me into the closet door as I gasp.

"You taste just like I remember," he grunts as he devours my neck with nips and licks.

"Hmmm." I tug at his shirt, and he leans away from me, his eyes dilated with desire. He pulls his shirt up and over his head in that sexy way only a man can do.

Once his shirt is discarded somewhere on the floor behind us, I waste no time running my fingers over the swirls of black down his arms and chest. I'm so enthralled with his ink. His chuckle is deep and throaty, and when I gaze into his eyes, he smirks.

"You want to lick them?"

Blinking, I wonder how he read my mind. He must see my confusion because he barks out a laugh. "Your note. I got the note you left in my hotel drawer."

The memory floods back to me as I bite my lip, and his eyes dart to the motion. "I thought the plan was to see if another guest of the room got it and wrote back," I say.

His eyes narrow on me, and something dark flashes in them. "So you meant to tell someone else you wanted to spend hours licking their tattoos?" His tone, I realize, is dripping in jealously. And I grin.

"Maybe." I lift my shoulder in indifference.

"You're gonna pay for that." He gently sets me down but doesn't step away as he nips my ear and digs his fingers into my sides. I burst out in a fit of giggles.

"Noo. Noooo. Stop." I laugh while his fingers hit all the ticklish spots I've long since forgotten about. "I hate being tickled."

"Then why are you laughing?" He chuckles. I twist and buck, and those damn giggles betray me over and over.

"Fine. I lied. I want to lick you," I shout through the laughter. His fingers stop, and I take my first deep breath in what feels like hours.

"You can lick me, Kel."

I blink through the tears of laughter, and I see his face is full of lust with no hint of laughter remaining. I start to say something, but the words die on my lips as he darts his tongue out and licks my lips. My breathing doesn't have a chance to even out after the laugh attack before I pull him back to me and devour his sinful mouth.

Barely breaking contact, he growls, "Condom, back pocket."

I reach around him, sliding my hand down to his ass and feeling for his wallet. But in the other pocket, I feel the condom and mutter, "That was easy."

"I thought it would be like this, Kelly," he whispers into my ear.

With my back wedged between his hard body and the door, I push my weight into the door as I unbuckle his belt and then unbutton his pants. As I unzip his pants, I realize I'm still clothed.

"My pants," I hiss.

He makes quick work of my shirt and shorts, making sure to take my panties with them. I reach for his jeans again and push them down, pleasantly surprised that he's not wearing any boxers. "Time saver?" I breathe as I rip open the condom. I'm trying my damnedest not to get sidetracked by his large cock as it springs forward between us, free of its confines.

His chuckle turns to a hiss as I grin up at him and slide the condom down his length. His eyes drift shut for a moment and then he lifts me up. My legs instinctively wrap around him as Ben presses me against the cool wall. I sensually run a finger from the top of his chest down over his abdomen. He reaches between us and grips his girth, pumping once, twice.

"Fuck," he draws out. "You're no longer in charge here, you evil woman."

That's when he takes over, lining himself up with my center and pushing in. I suck in a breath as he bottoms out, holding it while he stills inside me.

"You feel so fucking good, Kelly." He looks deep into my eyes, leaning in and kissing me stupid while he starts to move. Being with him like this is too much and not enough all at once. I've missed this, missed him. Everything around us ceases to exist as pleasure builds through my body. His name tumbles from my lips as I beg for more.

Ben slips his hand between my legs and finds my clit, circling the sensitive bud with his thumb and sending me over the edge. "So hot," he grunts as his thrusts quicken and then he stills, breathing heavy. "Goddamn, Kelly. I needed that."

We don't make it out to dinner that night. We stay in

and call for pizza instead of seeing the town like we planned. And Ben takes me again, this time slower. I can feel every ounce of emotion rolling off him in the process.

So much for *just friends*.

"SO, be honest, what did you think of Aubrey and Chance?" I twirl my straw around in my glass of iced tea as I look at Ben.

We found ourselves at a tiny hole-in-the-wall seafood place after one heck of a long day. Somehow, Ben and I were able to get out of bed and hit the beach early. We didn't surf for long, mostly because I knew Ben's still learning. Sometimes I can get carried away and spend hours on the waves.

We made it back with plenty of time to spare before brunch with Aubrey and Chance. Ben seemed to like them, and they both gave me their approval. Not that it matters since we're just friends. Then I showed him around Hermosa Beach and took him by the shelter to introduce him to some of my favorite furry friends.

The day has been utterly amazing. I'm trying not to think about how he's leaving tomorrow, and I'm not sure when I will see him again. I mentally shake myself away from that train of thought.

"They seem pretty cool." He nods his head. "They're in their thirties, yeah?"

I nod, confirming the slight age difference.

"They're protective of you," he says, his face serious.

"Oh, no. Who said what and when?" I straighten in my seat.

He chuckles and shakes his head. "I expected as much. Aubrey quietly—and not so subtlety—inferred she'd slice my neck if I hurt you. And Chance made it clear I'd hurt for weeks if I even so much as made you cry."

I blow out a breath. "Wow. I'm sorry about that. They know we're just friends." I bite on the inside of my cheek.

"Don't worry about it. They care about you. It makes me happy that you've got people looking out for you." His half-smile looks sadder than anything else.

"What about you? Do you have any one looking out for you out in Chicago?"

"Sure. I've got my teammates. And Garland here in Cali." He shrugs it off.

"What about your parents? I thought they were in Chicago as well." I lean my chin on my palm, leaning toward him.

"They are. We're good, but I'm busy and they don't understand the whole pro gaming thing. So I wouldn't say they're super active in my life. But it's fine." He snags a fry from his plate—there are only a few left—and drags it through the small dish of ketchup. I study him and I realize that he looks... sad.

"Are you happy, Ben?" I ask softly.

His eyes drag up to mine, and that cocky smirk falls into place. I immediately see it for what it is—a mask.

"Of course I'm happy." I narrow my eyes at him but say nothing. He continues. "Why wouldn't I be happy? I get to do what I love for a living, and I get paid well to do it. I've got friends and fans. I'm young and healthy. What's not to be happy about?" he leans back into his chair, stretching his legs out at an angle. He's the picture-perfect image of a relaxed, content male.

I don't believe it.

"Are you lonely?" I ask, barely above a whisper.

He ponders my question. Looking down at his feet for a moment, he says, "No." But when he slowly looks up at me, all traces of the cocky gamer that sat before me only seconds ago are gone. "Maybe," he mutters.

"Tell me," I urge.

"I don't know exactly when I realized that everything around me was changing." He moves forward, leaning his forearms on the table.

"How so?"

"The team, for one. As a whole, we're at the peak of our career. We're the team to beat. But it goes deeper than that. Like, there's always been girls hanging around since our name really got out there. But it's different now. The guys are settling down. Hell, Dex, our team captain, is getting married soon. Simon reconnected with his childhood best friend and they went from enemies to lovers like that." He snaps his finger. "It's only a matter of time before Bernie gets her happily ever after."

"I'd like to meet Bernie someday. She sounds like a badass." I laugh.

"She really is. She's got this mad crush on Dex's brother. That fool has got to either be blind or stupid not to see it," he grumbles.

"You're very observant." Tilting my head to the side, I try to read him.

"I see fucking everything," he tells me with conviction, as he looks deep into my eyes. I don't break the connection, even though there's a table between us.

From the corner of my eye, I see his Adam's apple bob as he swallows. "I see you too, Kel."

I nod. "Yeah? And what do you see?" I breathe.

"You're lonely, too. Just like me." I suck in a breath and wonder when I became such an open book.

"I thought you said you weren't lonely." I don't smile, concerned about how the mood turned somber.

His shoulder lifts in a shrug. "Maybe I lied."

I narrow my eyes at him, and he seems to know I don't like his response. He lets out a sigh. "More like... I just don't want to admit it."

Then tension in my neck eases. "What would make you less lonely?"

"You." His gaze fixes on mine. My body heats, and I run the risk of melting into a puddle of goo right here for everyone to see.

I work my jaw, making sure I have control over my body, "You've got me. Friends. Remember?"

His eyes darken. "And does anyone else have you, too?" he nearly growls.

Blinking back surprise, I tilt my head. "I don't understand. You said you didn't want a relationship. When did friendships become exclusive?"

Anger flashes in his eyes as he opens his mouth, but he must think better of what he was about to say because he snaps it shut instead. I narrow my eyes on him—I can almost guess what he was going to say.

"Are you sleeping with anyone else, Kel?" His tone is tight, clipped.

He's the one who didn't want a relationship, and suddenly, he doesn't want me sleeping with anyone else? I shake off my anger because I don't want to fight.

"No, Ben. Just you. My friend." I can't hide the bitterness, and he catches it.

"I don't like the idea of a long-distance relationship. I told you that from the start."

I cross my arms over my chest and lean back in my chair. "I'm not asking for one."

He leans closer, "You didn't let me finish. "I like the idea of you hooking up with anyone else even less," he bites out.

I raise a brow.

"What I'm saying is that I want to be more than friends with you, Kelly."

My heart hammers in my chest. "But…"

"I know what I said, Kelly. Last night, today—hell, the last few weeks—it all solidified that I want to give this a shot. It's not going to be easy, but I think we should try." His lips press together as he exudes calm.

My heart is anything but calm. "Okay," I let out on a shaky breath.

The tension that has him bound tight shatters as he lets out a soft, "Thank God."

I can't help but grin, my heart taking flight like a bird being let out of its cage. We stare at each other, all dopey-eyed grins.

Then he snickers before asking, "Does this mean your friends' warnings of my decapitation gets more vivid and elaborate now that I'm your boyfriend?"

Warmth spreads across my chest at the term boyfriend, even though I'm far too old to feel giddy about it. Snorting, I tell him the truth. "I have no idea, but I can imagine much more violent threats."

"You should visit me in Chicago. Meet my friends." He beams, and I nod in agreement. I'd pretty much agree to anything at this point.

That's when another truth hits me square in the chest.

Shit, this is gonna hurt like hell.

ELEVEN

Ben
―――

I pick up my phone and swipe to listen to the voicemail. Assuming the call was spam, I let it roll, but as I lie in bed trying to find sleep, I decide to listen.

"HELLO, Ben. This is Ronni from Gallant Gaming. We received your application for the Producer position. I would love to talk with you regarding the current opportunities we have available. I think you may be just who we're looking for. Please, give me a call."

SHE RATTLES off her number and the message ends. I let out a breath. I filled out that application weeks ago. I had almost written off the company. Gallant Gaming is one of the leading video game developers in the industry, and from what I hear, they're a great company to work for. I'm still not sure what I want to do, but I know I'm going to have to figure it out fast. I was hesitant to apply for this job because their headquarters is in New York. Born and raised in Chicago, I'm not sold on moving, but I need to keep my options open.

If I take this job in NYC, I'm going to face another big issue—moving even farther away from Kelly.

We've only been official for a few weeks now, but if we have any chance of a future together, I should consider this relationship when thinking of what's next in my career. The thought of moving even farther from her tugs at my heart a little too hard not to.

Kelly is amazing; the highlight of my day is talking to her. I'm always counting down the days until I see her next. If I move to NYC, then the already small amount of time we get to see each other will reduce. Short of me moving to Cali, I can't see how I'll be able to continue with our current setup. Working with Lasso on a contract basis allows me to visit her. But once I get a full-time gig after leaving the team, I'm going to have to save my visits to weekends only. Plus, they'll be random, and I'll zip through my frequent flyer miles quickly.

I scrub my hand down my face and toss my phone on the nightstand next to the bed.

Fuck.

I'm fucking lost right now. Pro gaming just fell into my lap. I'm stupid if I think my next job will, too.

I kick off the sheet, suddenly getting overheated in my bed. Punching my pillow, I roll to my side and blink at the wall.

I haven't talked to the team about moving on yet. I know it's only a matter of time before Dex and Simon do, but something's gnawing at me to move on first. I don't want to be left behind or stuck in a situation I didn't see coming. I see the ending to Team NoMad as it's coming, and I'm ready to embrace it.

Maybe I need to broach the situation with Dex and

Simon. Or talk to Bernie. I need to feel them out and get an idea of what they're thinking.

Then maybe after I do that, I need to talk to Kelly about what it means for us when I'm no longer enjoying free flights and frequent visits to Cali.

Would she be willing to move wherever I end up? We could live together, she could find a job, or I could support her for a while—no biggie. Would she leave her friends and family? Fuck, I don't think she would. She's really loving her job right now, and I know it's been a long time coming for her to find something she truly enjoys. No way could I ask her to uproot her life for me. We've known each other for a few months, and I've only been her boyfriend for a few weeks. We just aren't there yet. Unfortunately, this decision will come before we are.

I know if I had the opportunity, I'd move to Cali. But I've checked, and there aren't many career opportunities in my wheelhouse at the moment. I'd love to work at Lasso, but they aren't hiring. I've got enough money to keep me comfortable for a while, but I'm not the kinda guy who likes sitting around and doing nothing.

Her face flashes through my mind, and I'm hit with a pang of sadness. I don't want us to be over, but this long-distance thing is no joke. It's hard being here in the Windy City and her over in the Golden State. The three-hour time difference doesn't help. Oftentimes, I don't think about it and call her super early when she's still asleep. Or I call her when she's still working. It sucks, but it's something we'll have to get used to, I guess.

It takes me several minutes of lying in the dark before I fall asleep. And it feels like only moments have passed when I'm startled awake by the vibration coming from the nightstand.

Groggily, I reach over, patting around for my phone.

Opening one eye, I lift my phone and see it's Kelly. I also see that it's just past three in the morning.

"Hello?" My voice is gravelly with sleep. My eyes stay shut as I rest the phone on my face.

"Oh my God. You were asleep," she slurs.

"Yeah."

"Shit sticks, what time is it? I don't even know what time it is." She's drunk.

"It's three here," I mumble, still not awake.

"Ben, I'm so sorry. Aubrey and I went out for drinks, and I just got home and all I wanted to do was talk to you." She draws out the last word. I can picture her sitting on her bed, pouting.

"It's okay. You sound like you had a lot to drink. Did you have fun?" I smile in the dark when she giggles her response.

"So much fun, but way too much sex on the beach."

"As in the drink?" My dick stirs as I hear the word sex on her lips.

"Yes, silly. Who else would I be having sex on the beach with if you're there and I'm here?" More drunken giggles.

"Exactly." I roll to my back, dropping the phone on my face. I grab it quickly, and she's chatting about her night. While I'd love to be sleeping right now, hearing her voice is just as relaxing.

"I miss you." Her whisper fills the phone.

Frowning, I realize again just how damn much I miss her. "I miss you, Kel."

"I wish you were here with me tonight. I love my girl time with Aubs, but..." she trails off.

"How about next time we see each other, we go out? You can drink all the sex on the beach you want, and I'll be there with you."

"While I grope you all night." Her voice goes sultry and my dick twitches.

"Is that right? You get touchy and feely when you're tipsy, huh?" I chuckle.

"Only with you. All I can think about is that fucking hot bod of yours, gamer boy." She sighs. "Which, I'll be honest, I wasn't expecting your body to be so sexy, but I love it. Looooovve it," she purrs.

"Your body is fucking hot. Those surfer legs make me hard just thinking about them wrapped around me." I groan at the thought, covering my eyes with my hand.

She whimpers at my response.

"So not fair that you're here and I'm there," she whines.

A bubble of laughter rises up through my throat. "Kel, it's the other way around. I'm here, you're there."

"Whatever. Same difference." She goes quiet, and after a few moments, I wonder if she's still there. Then she speaks again. "Pixy is a really good goat, you know? Almost like a dog."

I smile into the darkened room. "You saying you want a goat?"

"No, I think the Bateman's got very lucky with their goat. Except for the fainting part," she replies.

"That is unfortunate. And also very odd."

She keeps on going about the goat. "I mean, he's not very soft. If I were to get a pet, it would have to be fuzzy and soft. I like snuggles. Cuddling is a passion of mine."

"I'll cuddle you," I tell her, hoping to hear her laugh again.

"Hmm."

"Kel?" I question.

The only response I get is a soft snore. My girl just passed the fuck out after telling me cuddling is her passion.

"Night, Kelly," I whisper into the phone before ending the call and going back to sleep.

DUE TO MY LATE NIGHT–ER, early morning—call from Kelly, I decide that coffee may not do the job today. I'm exhausted and I'm considering doing something I haven't done since college. A good ole fashion mid-day nap. Shutting down my computer in the training room, I figure out how much time I've got until my meeting with my financial planner this afternoon.

I took a page from Dex's book, and a couple of years ago when I was bringing in more money than I ever expected when it came to pro gaming, I hired a financial planner. I don't invest a lot, but mostly, my guy has saved me from wasting all my money. I have a call with him quarterly, but I set up a call today because I wanted to go through some numbers. If I stopped gaming at the end of this season, how long could I comfortably go without working? Or how long could I afford to freelance? Basically, I just wanted to get my shit together.

I've got two hours. While I doubt I'll manage to sleep for two hours—I've already had a shit-ton of coffee today—I have two hours to relax. Just as I get to the front door, I hear Dex call to me from the workout room.

"Ben, wanna grab a quick bite for lunch?" Looking over my shoulder, I see Dex walking toward me, Simon behind him.

I contemplate losing out on that nap just as my stomach rumbles. Screw the nap—I'll just get more coffee. "Yeah, sure."

Dex comes to my side and slaps my shoulder. "Awesome. Link is meeting us. Let's go."

Link is Dex's best friend and a famous YouTube star. He used to be on the team, but he retired a couple of years ago to focus on his YouTube empire. He's a good dude but cocky as shit. He lives with Simon upstairs, but he's still around and oftentimes forgets he's not actually on the team anymore.

The three of us make our way to a nearby bar we frequent often for lunch, dinner, and late-night drinks. It's like a second home. Waltzing in and taking a corner booth in the back to join Link, who's already made himself comfortable.

"Ladies, how are you today?" he sing-songs.

Rolling my eyes, I ignore him. I've found it's best to ignore the dude at times. The three guys, who I'll admit are thick as thieves, chat and talk about their morning. I've often wondered what it would be like to have such close friends. Not only are they close, but all of their girlfriends are close, too. It's like some strange little family of couples. If it weren't for Bernie, I'd feel like the awkward man out. Don't get me wrong, the ladies in these guys' lives are all wonderful, but I tend to stay away from group settings.

These three have one another's backs. They know each other well and are always up in one another's business. *No, thank you.* My closest friend is Garland, and we live thousands of miles apart. Still, in the back of my mind, I always sort of thought I should have tried a little harder to get into this little family. It's water under the bridge at this point. I'm going to leave the team soon and they will all, in some way, still be together.

"So what's up with you, Ben? Haven't seen ya around," Link says from across the booth.

"Just chilling. I've been going to Lasso a lot, working on some voice-overs." I take a drink of the Diet Coke the server just dropped off. We come here so often that the servers know our drink orders.

"That's right. Lasso is epic. I've worked with them before. Awesome company." He nods.

"Are you planning on working with them more?" Dex asks this time, and I glance in his direction, trying to figure out if he's on to me.

"Maybe. I really like the work. But it's all freelance right now. Works with the schedule nicely." Truth.

"Well, I wouldn't be surprised if they try to snag you up full time one of these days." He grins, and I realize that now would be the time to do a little digging.

I lean on to the table, my forearms flush with the top. "Have you ever thought about what you'll do when you retire from the team?" I don't sugarcoat it—I just throw it out there and hope I catch something.

Dex chuckles and Simon sneers.

"Oh, real talk time, boys." Link claps his hands with glee. I snort at his excitement. *What an idiot.*

"Sure, I have," Dex answers. "Have you?"

I assess him, wondering if he's been wanting to bring this up with me, and I've just offered up the ideal time to do it.

"Not sure." I look over to Simon. Both he and Link are relaxed, and I decide this could be an easy conversation. Easier than expected, at least. "I don't know. I've got an itch recently..."

Link interjects. "Maybe get it checked out, man."

I flip him off, and my tablemates chuckle as I continue. "Just an urge to figure out what I'm going to do next—whenever that may be."

"I get it. We've," Dex motions to the whole table, "all gotten to live and breathe our passion. But we can't do this forever. Eventually, we all have to 'grow up.'" He air quotes the last words.

"Speak for yourself, douche. I'm never growing up," Link sputters.

"This is exactly why we don't include Link in serious, adult conversations." Simon shakes his head and Link just grins.

"I've got a plan," Dex says, lifting his shoulder like it's not a big deal.

"You're getting married. I would think that's probably wise," I tell him.

"I know I want to do some game design with that art degree I have collecting dust," Simon throws out.

"You probably could design games, degree or not," Dex says, and it's true. Simon is wicked good at design. Any gaming company would want him in a heartbeat.

"What are you thinking?" Dex asks.

Shrugging, I say, "I don't know. I think I'd like to manage the development of a game. I really like the narrating, though."

"Shit, Ruby and Bernie listen to all those romance audiobooks. You should look into doing that." Link laughs, but I've heard that before.

"Believe it or not, you're not the first one to suggest that."

"I can see it now. All those ladies losing their minds as you read the sexy scenes in those novels. Instant orgasms," Link says. He's a tool, but I one-up him.

"Yeah, can you imagine Ruby sitting on the couch next to you, me whispering a dirty sex scene in her ear? Getting all hot and bothered, and you having absolutely nothing to do with it." I grin at his shocked face. Simon and Dex silently lose it next to him.

"Fuck. You're an asshole," he fusses, and we all laugh.

We get our meals and start to eat. Talking about upcoming tournaments and Link's newest videos. And because they're all hopelessly in love, their girlfriends make their way into the conversation.

"How's Kelly?" Dex asks.

"She's good. She's actually visiting next weekend."

"What? We get to meet surfer girl Kelly?" Link puts his burger down.

I shake my head. "I didn't say that. I said she's visiting, not meeting you." I point my fork at him.

"Come on man. You know the girls are gonna want to meet her."

"That's fine. But it's still not happening for you, man." Fuck, I don't care if she meets the whole crew, but I love giving him a hard time.

He glares at me as if he's wounded.

"I'm looking forward to meeting her," Dex adds. And I wonder what she's going to make of this tight-knit crew I'm barely a part of. I wonder if she'll see right through it. That I'm a loner and she can do way better than me. I grumble away the thoughts and try to get back into the easy conversation around me.

Later, when we're heading back to the apartment, Dex pulls me back while Simon and Link walk ahead of us.

"I want to invest. There was a small gaming company looking for backers that came to me with this online game idea. So I jumped in, and I'm going to help them get their game out there. It's going to be massive. They're going to need people in this business who know a thing or two to help them navigate the success they're going to have, and I want to be there to do just that."

His truth comes out of nowhere when I realize he's telling me he's already started to move on.

"That sounds like a solid plan, Dex."

"Whenever you're ready to move on, don't think for one second you're going to upset us. We're all there, man. The end is near, and you're not the only one looking toward the future." His words permeate as Simon says something to us over his shoulder. Dex gives me a knowing grin before replying to Simon.

The rest of my day—fuck it, the rest of my week—I think about what he said.

It's time to move on, and all those feelings of not wanting to be left behind—well, I'm not an idiot for feeling them. Now if only I can figure how to navigate making massive career changes and being in a long-distance relationship at the same time.

TWELVE

Kelly

Navigating my way through O'Hare, I make my way through terminal two. I didn't bother with a suitcase. Everything I needed for the weekend fit into an overnight bag I used as my second carry-on. So, after making my way off the plane, my time is only spent figuring out how to get out of this busy place. Ben told me he'd be waiting for me near the entrance, and I'm eager to see him. It's been a month. All the calls, texts, and occasional FaceTime just weren't enough. I want to feel him, smell him. I want to see him face to face without a screen between us.

Imagining him waiting for me, I wonder if things will be awkward between us. Is going so long between visits going to make our time together even sweeter, or will it strain our relationship?

All I want—no, need—is to be close enough for his musky scent to make my head swim with the heady intoxication I am now used to feeling when we're together.

The automatic glass doors at the front of the airport catch my attention first. The glass must be tinted because the sun shining in doesn't cast shadows over the many people milling about. I scan the groups of people looking for the dark, tattooed gamer I know is waiting. His text came through just as I stepped foot into the lobby off the plane.

That's when my eyes land on Ben. A breath catches in my throat as I take in the dark jeans, Cubs T-shirt, and all that glorious artwork up and down his thick arms. My mouth waters before I check myself. *You're in public, Kelly.* It'd be smart to remember that. But when his gaze meets mine, his cocky grin unleashes my own answering smile, and he starts toward me. His stride is confident and I bite back a moan. He's close enough now that when he opens his mouth, I hear him growl, "Get over here, Kel."

I fling myself forward. One step, two, three—and I'm in his open arms. My feet leave the ground, and I'm utterly lost in him. His body wrapped around mine, I breathe him in, and his arms tighten around me. Felling his lips on my neck, I rub my nose against the softness behind his ear.

"Fuck. I missed you," he says into my hair.

Tears form behind my eyes and emotion threatens my voice. "I missed you, too." I squeeze him closer and force those tears away. *I will not cry.* I'm happy to see him, but the desperation of missing him is overwhelming now that he's here and in my arms.

How do people handle long-distance relationships? I can't even handle a month. Shame mixes with embarrassment as they try to fight their way past my excitement of being here, but I win the war and plaster a smile on my face as he sets me back on solid ground and leans away to study me.

"Welcome to Chicago. I'll be your guide for the weekend. Your wish is my command." He grins.

"Promise?" I giggle, unashamed.

"Always." Heat fills his eyes, and I contemplate making

my first wish to find an empty closet or unoccupied family restroom somewhere so I can show him exactly how badly I missed him. But I'm a fucking lady, so I practice restraint and settle for a kiss.

Lifting up on my toes, I plaster a kiss on his warm lips. I feel his grin as he kisses me back. When he breaks the kiss, I can't help but push my bottom lip out in a pout. Chuckling, he grabs the bag I don't remember dropping to the ground beside us. Shouldering it, he grabs my hand and pulls me toward the sliding glass doors.

"There will be plenty of time for that later, baby. I'm not one to put on a show." He looks over at me, and I can tell by his look, he'd be tempted to had I fought him on ending that kiss.

We wait several moments for an available taxi.

"Did you not drive here?" I ask as he motions for me to get in the car first.

My bag follows me in and then he folds himself into the seat next to me, closing the door. He tells the cabbie where to take us before answering me.

"I don't have a car. When you live downtown, you just use public transportation. The L train, cabs, Uber. Take your pick."

"Doesn't it get expensive?" I muse as I take in the sights out the window.

"Nah. The L Train and bus are less than three bucks a ride. And most people buy transit cards so they don't have to fish out a couple of bucks from their pockets to pay for their rides. I walk a lot, too."

Interesting. Big city life, I guess. But I've never spent much time in big cities, so this is all new to me.

"Can you surf here in Chicago?" I wonder out loud.

"You didn't bring your board." He chortles.

Turning to him, I smile. "No, I did not. I just wasn't

sure. Oceans are by far the best bodies of water for surfing, in my humble opinion, but I didn't know if people ever surfed on Lake Michigan."

His expression is blank as he contemplates his answer. "They do. There's a beach on fifty-seventh that's great for surfing in the spring and fall, but I've never surfed here. In Chicago."

"Huh," is all I say before looking back out the window. A quietness falls between us, and I wonder what he's thinking about that has his lips pressed together, a slight grimace on his face.

Clearing my throat, I ask, "So what's the plan for this weekend?"

He shakes away whatever got him stuck in his own mind. "I'm gonna show you around Chicago and then introduce you to some of my friends. But mostly, I have plans for you in my bed, for several hours at a time."

I gulp back a moan as need slams into me. As if he can sense my desire, he leans across the seat and kisses my neck. Tilting my head to give him better access, he breathes me in, and my eyes flutter closed.

I'm sitting in the back of a cab.

We must be on the same wavelength, or I muttered the words out loud, but he groans and pulls himself away from me.

I find more Chicagoland questions to ask him to keep us from mauling each other until we arrive at what I assume to be his apartment.

"Let's drop off your bag in my apartment and then I'll show you where I spend most of my days." He places a hand on my lower back as we walk toward the impressive building.

"The training room?" I guess.

"Yup. I'll bet you money even though we called it quits

for the day two hours ago, people are waiting around to meet you." His brow is furrowed.

"And that's a bad thing?" I hedge.

"No, it's just—I keep to myself and these people..." He waves his hand toward the elevator we're walking to.

"Your teammates?" I offer.

"Yeah, they're nosy assholes and they like to gossip." His wrinkled nose causes me to grin.

"And me being here is worthy gossip?" I don't quite understand his grumpiness, but it's cute as hell.

"No, it's just, somehow, they're all up to speed on you and it's unsettling to me."

"Because you keep to yourself?" I get it. And he's adorable.

"It's Bernie's fault, really. Well, and Garland's," he grumbles. Then under his breath, I hear a muttered, "Fucking Garland Thorpe."

"Well, I appreciate the need and want to not share every aspect of your life with someone. Remember, my best friend is as nosy as they come, but I'm looking forward to meeting your friends. They clearly care about you."

He grumbles a little more as we step onto the elevator, but his answering kiss surprises me and all talk of nosy friends is forgotten about.

All too soon, we're in his apartment. I'm being herded down a short hall and pushed into a bedroom. The scent of Ben, the one I spend my nights trying to conjure in my mind, fills my senses. His bed is pushed against the wall, and I have just enough time to notice the desk on the other side of the room with two computer screens and a large comfy looking desk chair before he's pushing me toward his bed.

His shirt is ripped up and off, leaving his bare, sculpted chest the only thing I see. His rough hands find the hem of my own shirt as he quickly drags them up my body. His knuckles leave goosebumps in their wake. My shirt is off and tossed aside, then his hands reach for my shorts.

"I got it," I tell him, pushing his hands toward his own jeans. I kick off my shoes as I unfasten my pants and push them down until just past my knees, and they slide right to the floor. That's when my focus is back on him as he pounces on me, and I let out a squeal.

"A month is too long," he growls before he buries his face between my swollen breasts, leaving a hot trail of wet kisses in his path.

Moaning, I pull at his hair, needing his mouth. Once I have his lips back on mine, I don't even care that I sound like a sex-starved animal. That's exactly what I am. This man does this to me.

He pulls away and peppers kisses down my chin and to my neck, then he's kissing my chest again. His molten attention doesn't stop as he works his way down my tummy as he licks right above the seam of my lace undies.

He's not gentle as he shoves his fingers under the fabric—he's rushed. And so am I as I lift my hips. He pulls at the only remaining layer between his mouth and me.

I watch with rapt attention as he runs his hands up my legs, spreading them further apart. An instant later, he runs his tongue along my sensitive flesh before sucking my clit into his mouth.

I cry out, fingers mindlessly finding his hair. Several minutes pass with his mouth on my center, his hand over my abdomen, pushing me into the bed, keeping me still.

Just as I'm about to shatter, he rips himself away. "Fuck. I want it all, Kelly. But I need to be inside you. Right now."

"Please," I breathe in a whimper.

I don't know where or when he grabbed it, but he rolls

on a condom, and my breathing stops as he plunges into me. No teasing, no easing into it. He just takes what we both so desperately need.

I'm so close to breaking that I moan out when he slams back into me. Over and over, I feel the tug, and I ignore that my heart and soul—my entire being—is drawn to this man buried deep inside me. Lust can be a wicked bitch, and I'm not going to let myself think about how the heart often confuses lust and love in moments like this.

His lips find mine, and the kiss isn't sexy and sweet. It's messy and dirty, and I want more of it. Wrapping my legs around his waist, I dig my heels into his ass, pulling him tighter. My nails claw at his shoulders as I arch into his kiss.

His movement becomes more and more frantic, and I moan as I feel my walls start to break. Burying himself deep one final time, I shiver as my body bursts into a million tiny pieces. Ben falls over the edge only seconds after.

With deep, staggering breaths, we try to calm our racing hearts.

"Fuck, I missed you, Kelly." He lets out a humorless laugh. As if he's almost angry.

He's lying on top of me, and there's nowhere I'd rather be. But in this moment, I worry he's not as happy about us uniting as I am. I kiss his cheek, feeling him let out another ragged breath.

"I'm sorry if I was rough," he whispers.

"It was just what I wanted," I whisper back.

He pushes up on his forearm, his eyes searching mine. I smile, telling him I'm fine. Finally, he smiles back. The Ben I know and am falling in love with is staring back at me. His cocky smirk and the gleam in his eye melt my brain and all logical thought.

Looking into his handsome face, I realize that raging

hearts and stupid thoughts cause nothing but unbearable heartache. That's the path I'm heading down if I don't check myself and gather my wits. Ben Ford will break my heart and it hurts like hell knowing it's coming.

AFTER OUR QUICKIE in Ben's room, we right ourselves, and I fix my sex-mused hair before we leave his apartment and walk down the hall to the training room. Calling it a training room feels insignificant once I take a step inside and realize how expansive the space is. I remember him saying it was two apartments in one—but, wow, this space is impressive.

I mumble the word, and he chuckles in reply.

"Yeah, it is." He takes my hand, shutting the door behind him.

My name rings out from a feminine voice. My head whips to the left as Ben grumbles. There's a plush and leather seating area where three ridiculously attractive people sit. A female jumps up from her perch on the chair, and two guys lounge on the couch. His teammates, who I recognize from the website—which honestly doesn't do any of them justice.

The woman walking toward me is wearing jeans with a few rips in them, and a T-shirt with several succulents on them that says, "what the fucculent" on it. I smile as she nears. Her long, dark brown hair hangs halfway down her back, and she's wearing clear, plastic, full-rimmed glasses. She could be Zoe Deutch's doppelganger, for sure.

"Hi, I'm Bernie." She pulls me into a hug, and there's something about her that has me going willingly. "I've heard so much about you."

"Come on, Bern, you're gonna scare her," one of the gamers behind her says.

She lets me go and just smiles at me.

"I've heard a lot about you, too," I tell her as she squeezes my hand before tugging me toward the couch. "Because Ben's a slacker, I'll make the introductions."

Ben grunts behind me but follows me.

She lifts a hand to the guys, and they briefly stand for introductions. "This is Dex and Simon. I'm sure you've heard their names—they piss Ben off a lot."

Laughing, I offer, "Not as much as a guy named Link." Then I look around for more people. All of them laugh and Ben wraps an arm around my shoulder.

"He has a way of annoying just about everyone he comes into contact with," the blond guy, Simon, says.

"How was your flight?" Bernie asks as she drags me to the other end of the massive couch and pulls me down onto it. Ben trails behind but opts for the recliner adjacent to us.

"Long. But easy," I tell her. I like her instantly. She's kind and happy and so eager to get to know me.

"Is Ben going to show you around the city? Wait. Have you been to Chicago before?"

I nod and start to say something, but Ben cuts in. "Give her a moment to breathe, Bern. Yes, I'm going to take her out to see the city."

Bernie offers me a bemused smile as I answer her last question. "I'm a Chicago newbie."

"You'll love it," she states with confidence.

"As much as a surfer girl can love a big city, though," Simon quips and Dex elbows him. Bernie's smile doesn't falter, so I ignore the comment. But in the corner of my eyes, I see Ben's nostrils flare as he stares down Simon in a cold, hard glare.

Cocky Gamer

"So if you have time while you're here, I would love for you to meet my friends. Morgan, Gia, and Ruby are super fun, you'll love them." Bernie smiles expectantly.

"Honestly, I'm surprised the whole gang isn't here," Ben answers gruffly.

Dex chuckles. "They wanted to be, man. But we didn't want to overwhelm Kelly."

"It would have been fine," I offer at the same time Ben grumbles, "Thank God."

Before long, Ben excuses us from the training room with promises of meeting up with the whole gang tomorrow for dinner. I say my goodbyes and follow Mr. Grumpy Gamer out into the hall.

"Let's go for a walk. Do you need anything?" he grunts, and I consider dragging him down to his apartment and trying to persuade him to leave the grouchiness at the door. But instead, I shake my head. I have my small purse hanging across my body still, and we walk silently to the elevator.

It's not until we've walked about a block away from the building that he starts to lighten up. I use this as the perfect opportunity to ask what the deal was back there. We've never been anything but embarrassingly honest with each other, so why should I hide my own feelings about the shift in his personality?

With his hands shoved in his pockets, he nods as if he was expecting my question.

"I've got some things on my mind. And, I *was* excited for you to meet my friends. Until they decided to point out how different our lives are and Bern tried to keep you all to herself. I guess I got a little possessive back there. I'm sorry." He looks over at me, smile wavering as he waits for my response.

A laugh bubbles out of me, and I shake my head. I

reach out and thread my hand under his arm, leaning into his side. "You have nothing to worry about, Ben. I'm all yours; you don't need to share."

He lets out a relieved sigh and leans into me, kissing my temple. He gets chattier the closer we get to the areas he wants to show me. In the end, the night is pleasant, and his grumpy behavior with his teammates is just a fleeting memory.

The next day is filled with much of the same as the afternoon before. Sex, sightseeing, more sex, and more sightseeing. An hour before we are due to meet his friends for dinner, he gets a call and excuses himself down the hall, leaving me sitting on his bed.

My eyes wander around his room, and it's obvious that everything he owns is crammed into this small room. I can't stop thinking about what it would be like if we lived together someday—if fate brought us together in a more permanent way, and his game stuff mixed in with my surf stuff and all my books I'm obsessive about.

I mean, how long can a couple really keep up a long-distance relationship before settling down somewhere and making it official? Suddenly, I understand Ben's worry from last night. Would he move to Hermosa or Culver City? Would I move here? Ugh, do I want to live in Chicago? The city is beautiful, but I'm a beach girl through and through. Would I be able to give all that up for a man? Would I move this soon into a relationship? If Ben asked me to, would I?

Maybe.

Just as my thoughts spiral out of control—I mean, I'm one step away from doodling my name plus his on every empty spot in an imaginary notebook—Ben walks back in.

"Everything good?" I ask, noticing his face is tight.

"Yeah." He starts to say more but stops as he sits in his gamer chair.

"How was it?" I push. The call is clearly bothering him.

"It was a call about a job I applied for." His voice is sharp, and I consider leaving it at that, but that's not who I am. I don't shy away from awkwardness.

I straighten. "Okay, so it wasn't good news?"

"No, it was."

"All right," I draw out. "Well, something is wrong. Tell me about the job."

His jaw tightens then relaxes before he speaks. "It would be a great opportunity for me. It's too soon to say anything else."

I nod and he stares down at the phone in his hands.

"Well, I'm gonna go get ready for dinner," I offer. I gather my hair and makeup bag and as I pass, he snatches my hand. Looking down at him, I see the worry in his eyes, but he smiles anyway.

"I'm sorry for being a dick. I'm just stressed out."

"Okay," I respond.

"Really. It's not you." He pulls me closer to him.

Leaning down, I kiss him on the nose. "I'm here to talk or listen whenever you need, Ben." Then I kiss him on the side of his mouth and pull away and walk to his bathroom to get ready.

I'd love to say the night got easier, but that would be a lie. No, the night was strained, and if Ben's friends noticed it, they were kind enough not to let on. He was distant and quiet. He held my hand and talked when necessary, but he wasn't a wonderful date. He let his friends entertain me, and at the end of the night, I felt like I had gained four new girlfriends and lost one boyfriend.

Maybe I misread this whole relationship. Things

between us seem to be going alarmingly well. We're unable to keep our hands to ourselves when we're in the same room. We text and call at all hours of the day and night. I know there are times when relationships move fast. Not all adults take years to fall in love and get their happy ending, much like Aubrey and Chance. But I don't want to rush. And I feel like that's all I've done with Ben since that day outside Melting Moon when I spilled my coffee all over him.

Was Ben telling me the truth the night before? Does he regret my visit? Was he not ready for me to meet his people? It's all too much as I lie in bed next to him. His back is to me, and just as I did after his phone call, I feel like he's shut me out.

I fly out tomorrow at two in the afternoon. We haven't talked about the next time we'll see each other. And as I fall into a restless sleep, I wonder if him dropping me off at the airport tomorrow will be for the last time. I hate to get so damn deep in my head, but damn it, I wanted this too much.

Like I said, I knew it would hurt.

THIRTEEN

Ben

Kelly doesn't say much on the drive to the airport. As we got in the Uber outside my apartment, she told me I didn't have to come to the airport with her, that she could handle sitting in the back of a car by herself. But I wasn't ready to say goodbye to her yet, and I didn't know when I would see her again. So I climbed in behind her and sat quietly next to her. I was an ass yesterday—to her and the team. I woke up this morning ready to apologize, but her demeanor toward me changed.

Not that I can blame her. Still, I wanted to redeem what I could and end this visit on a high note, so I did the only thing I knew to make it better.

I tried waking her up by peppering kisses on her neck, hoping to apologize without any words, but she blew me off. Kelly claimed she had a headache and didn't sleep well, so I took that as a sign to give her space instead.

Tail tucked between my legs, I located some pain reliever and a glass of water for her, but that didn't seem to help either. She lit up a bit when Bernie stopped by to see her. But her mood soured again the minute Bernie left.

I clearly managed to drive a wedge between us after that call from Gallant Gaming yesterday, now damn if I knew the right way to fix things. I should have just told her exactly what was going on. That seemed like the adult thing to do, but I was holding back out of fear.

I wanted as much time with Kelly as I could get before it was time for her to leave, but things were strained. Gallant called about flying me out to meet with them, wanting me to meet the team and see the headquarters. Setting up a time to visit soon is their top priority. But I've got to look at my schedule and figure out if I want to put all this time and effort into this job. I don't want to waste their time—and mine—if I'm not actually considering taking the job. Do I really want to live in New York?

There's just a lot of shit in my head that I need to work through, and like the stubborn asshole I am, I've already decided I need to figure it out all on my own. The car pulls up to the airport at the second terminal, much like it did only two days ago. Slowly, we climb out of the car, and I shoulder her duffel. She's mad at me, but I don't let that keep me from grabbing her hand as we weave through the throngs of people milling about.

There are still no words between us as we arrive at the gates that tell me I can't go any further. She stops a few paces ahead of me before turning around and facing me. Her face remains blank.

She isn't much shorter than my five-nine, the top of her head coming to my chin. Looking down at her, I search her face for something—anything. But she doesn't look me in the eye.

"Look, Kel. I'm sorry for the way I acted yesterday."

She just looks at me, expecting me to continue. "I've got a lot of shit to figure out, and well, I just need some space to do that."

"Space," she repeats slowly.

"Yeah."

"There's about to be two thousand miles between us. I'd call that space." She doesn't smile as she looks down and grips her duffel tight. I don't know how to respond, so I tilt my head slightly to see if she's going to say anything more. She doesn't.

"My life is about to change drastically, and I need to figure out my plan before it's too late," I say, telling her what she already knows.

"I'm not sure I understand what that all means, but it's fine. Good thing I'm heading home, then."

"No, Kel, it's not a good thing you're heading home. Especially not like this." I sigh and drop my head. "I hate long distance. This seems like it would be so much easier if we didn't live so far apart. I know I screwed up, okay? I clearly suck at this whole thing, but I'm not ready to let you go." An announcement for her flight comes over the PA, and she looks over her shoulder toward the gates.

"Call me when you get home, yeah?" I lift my hands to her shoulders, gaining her attention. When she finally looks at me, I'm startled by the sadness I see in her eyes.

"I will," she mumbles. I pull her into a hug, and at first, she just stands there. But then she drops her duffel, her arms wrapping around me. I lean my head on top of hers and breathe her in. *Fuck, this feels like a final goodbye.*

I don't have it in me to ask her if that's exactly what this is. I just need to figure out where my life is heading. That includes my career, where I live, and what relationship it entails. I told her from the get-go that long-distance relationships weren't my jam. If I move even further away, it wouldn't be fair to either of us to continue down the path.

"I'm sorry," I whisper into her hair.

"I know," I barely hear her mumble.

"We will figure this out, Kel."

She pulls away first, leaning down and scooping up her bag. She gives me a tight-lipped smile and turns and walks away. Not once does she glance over her shoulder at me. And I feel the invisible string that connects us pulling taut and nearly breaking.

I consider calling out her name but decide that letting her go now will be easier than dragging this on.

Fuck. What am I saying?

Is this the end of the road for me and Kelly? Maybe we just need a couple of days to get our heads on straight.

A COUPLE of days turns into a week. Ten days ago, I dropped my girlfriend off at this same spot, but instead of stopping at the gates, I continue through them. I'm heading to Gallant Gaming for a quick trip. And then from New York, I'm heading to Los Angeles for E3, a yearly convention. Team NoMad was asked by VisionWave, the makers of *Call of Battle*, to attend as their guests. So this means we do a few signings and meet up with our sponsors. We also get to try out new games and sit through press conferences and such. Maybe it sounds boring, but to a gaming nerd, it's the hottest place to be every June. Plus, there's a new gaming system launching at the end of the year, and Team NoMad is on the schedule to try it out. The perks of this job are undeniable. Being part of the number one pro gaming team makes the deal even sweeter.

My flight to New York is eventless. I'm picked up by the assistant of my contact, Ronnie, at Gallant. He's a nice guy, overly excited about meeting me, and soon I learn that it's the whole team that's excited for my visit. Gallant takes up three floors in an office building that has twenty. The tour I get is in depth, and every single person I meet is friendly and welcoming.

Over lunch, I meet with several people I'm told I'd be working with. That's when I realize they aren't interested in hiring me for the job I applied for, Release Manager. Which I'm fine with, as that job wasn't exactly what I wanted in the first place. But now they want to hire me as their Online Community Manager—running their social media and blog, and handling community relations. And, damn, that's not what I'm looking for at all.

I tell them I'm only on Twitter because I have to be, and they reply that it doesn't matter. Every tweet I post would garner engagement within minutes of it posting, but then it should be ignored. I tell them I have no experience dealing with social media, and they reply that it isn't important to do this job.

They don't get it. They don't get that, while I appreciate the fans, they aren't what drives me to be the best. I love the industry. I love all the ins and outs—being involved from start to finish in the game's development is where I want to be.

I tell them this, and they respond that if I take the job as their Online Community Manager, I could make a switch to another department. Eventually.

I get it. I do. I'm just a pro gamer. My degree in product management doesn't give them the confidence they need to believe I'd be an asset to their team. My years of experience in a gamer role isn't enough of a "deep understanding" of how a video game is made. They want to put me in an easy role and see what I'm capable of. They want to use my reach and connections to pull in more fans and customers.

I spend the day at Gallant. I dig the company—the atmosphere and the people—even if I'm not sold on this position they're offering.

They lay out the compensation and benefits package. It's impressive, I'll give them that. They tell me the job goes live online in three weeks and needs to be filled before the end of the year. They understand I have obligations to my team until the end of August. I can accept the job and ease into it, not starting full time and in-person until September. I have anywhere from three weeks to two months to make my decision. If I don't decide to take the job before the job goes up online, I risk losing it. Though, Ronnie made it clear I'd still be at the top of the list.

I spend my flight to LA looking over the paperwork they gave me. It's a good deal. I'm just not one I'm sure I want to take. Is it worth moving my life to New York? Is it a job worth ending whatever's between Kelly and I? This is all the shit I'm going to have to mull over. I don't want to lose Kelly, but the more I read through the offer, the more I realize how hard the added distance is going to be. I hate this.

Since Kelly left Chicago, things between us have been strained. We text every day, but not nearly as much as we normally do. A lot of calls are missed. I can't figure out why I haven't told her I'm going to be so close to Hermosa. Why have I defaulted into asshole mode? I want to touch her and kiss her, but I'm hesitant. I'm starting to push her away, and I don't understand why. Ultimately, I decide to get through this busy-ass weekend before talking to Kelly about where we stand. My trip to Gallant is nearly forgotten two days later. It's been a busy two days, and the trade show is on fire this year. I make it a point to avoid the Gallant Gaming booth. I'm not a coward, it's just something I don't want to deal with.

We've got two more days here, and I'm trying to embrace it. I know whatever I'm doing next year will still bring me to E3, but I won't be here as a gamer. I won't be here as a coveted guest. I'm okay with that, but I decide to live it up.

Standing behind a black backdrop in one of the large convention rooms, I take in the scene. The team is getting ready for what has become our annual E3 signing. The large room is packed, but we can't see the line. The backdrop is long, and we were ushered in only moments ago through an entrance directly behind the fabric wall. I know on the other side of that wall is a large sign with our team's name and logo. Two long tables stretch in front of it where each of us—Chuck, myself, Bernie, Dex, and Simon—will take a seat. And for the next hour, we'll meet and greet fans and sign posters, photos, shirts, and game boxes. E3 is mostly only open to industry professionals and media outlets, but there are certain events, such as signings that are open to the public.

Right as an MC introduces us, I realize I haven't heard from Kelly in a couple of days. Pulling out my phone, I send her a quick text. I realize she texted me this morning and I never texted her back, and shame overwhelms me.

ME: Hey. Sorry I missed your text. It's been a crazy busy week.

Me: How are you? I miss you.

"PLEASE WELCOME TEAM NOMAD!" I hear over the PA and clapping hands and yells ensue. I pocket my phone and follow the rest of my team out to the table. I don't pull my phone back out of my pocket until we're ushered through the entrance of a small meeting room we've been given as our team's home base for the duration of the convention.

"Well, that was fun," Dex says with a chuckle.

They all chat about what's up next, but I'm not paying attention to them when I see my texts were undeliverable. Glancing at the corner of my screen, I see I have zero signal.

Well, shit.

"Ben, you want to grab lunch?" I look up at Simon and see he's the only one left in the room with me.

Shoving my phone back into my pocket, I say, "Where did everyone else go?"

Chuckling, Simon slaps my back as he pushes me out of the room and closes the door behind him.

"Dex has a lunch meeting. Bernie's off to find Link and Ruby for something. That leaves me and you. Let's get something to eat. I'm fucking starving."

"All right," I mumble. Wow, I totally zoned out and missed all of that.

Twenty minutes later, we have subs, chips, and drinks and find a table in one of the large makeshift cafeterias.

"So you visited Gallant a couple of days ago. How'd it go?" Simon says around a bite of his sandwich.

"The company is fire. Great atmosphere, welcoming team," I tell him honestly.

"I sense a *but* coming."

"But... they don't want me for the job I applied for. They want to hire me as their Online Community Manager." I take a drink of my orange soda.

Simon tilts his head. "And that's not what you're looking for?"

"Fuck, no. You know I'm only on Twitter because Rob said I had to pick one social media outlet—

marketability or some shit like that," I grunt. I pushed back on the social media crap. Management wanted me to be on Twitter, Instagram, Facebook, and either Twitch or YouTube. I made it clear I'm not interested in making videos or posting pictures about the food I eat for lunch. So I settled on Twitter. The whole team tweets, we have a Facebook page, and Bernie handles our team's Instagram account along with her personal one. Over the years, I've gotten used to Twitter, not minding it at all. But a few 280-character tweets a day work just fine for me.

"So you're not gonna take the job?" Simon asks, and I ignore the fact I haven't actually told the team I'm looking for other work and planning on leaving them.

I let out a deep sigh. "I don't know. It seems to be my only option."

"What does Kelly think?" he asks as he pops open his bag of pickled-flavored kettle chips.

I slide my gaze a few tables away. "I haven't told her."

"We've been busy. E3 and Comic-Con always suck all the energy out of you," he offers.

But I offer more truth, which is fucking hard, I like to keep my cards close to my chest. "No, I mean I haven't told her about the job." I suck down the rest of my soda.

"She's your girlfriend, man." He leans back in his seat, studying me. Then he shakes his head.

"I know," I grumble as I pick up a barbecue chip from the bag. "She knows there's a job offer, I just didn't tell her anything about it."

"Or that taking it would put even more miles between you." He shakes his head in disbelief some more.

"Yeah."

He leans forward. "Fuck, Ben, that's a bad move. Take it from someone who was in a relationship that didn't have honesty about career paths and goals. You gotta keep things open. Make decisions together."

"We haven't been a couple for long. It feels premature to talk about career changes, possible moves, and whatnot. She's not going to move to Chicago or New York."

He crosses his arms over his chest. "She say that?"

"No. But I don't want her to think she even has to consider it," I growl.

Simon doesn't back down. "What about California? There are a shit-ton of gaming companies that have made that state home. You could make the move there."

"We both agreed to a long-distance relationship, Simon," I mutter as I ball up the empty sandwich wrapper.

"So you aren't interested in being together in the same town then." It's not a question. And honestly, this conversation has me pissed off.

"I really like Kelly, but our lives are extremely different. And I have to think about what's best for myself right now."

His eyes bulge. "Wow. Douchewaffle alert."

"Yeah, I know." I scrub my hand down my face. "I know."

"Look. I'm not giving you career or relationship advice, but I'll say this—don't let a girl worth keeping around get away because you're too much of a coward to admit she's worth it. If you don't want that job, then pass on it. Don't force yourself into a situation you don't like because you feel you're out of options. You're not. You have time and choices."

"That sounds a lot like both relationship and career advice, Si," I tell him.

He lifts a shoulder before pushing back in his chair. We gather our trash from the table, and I lean over to pick up a napkin off the floor as my phone falls out of my side pocket. It tumbles to the floor right as a group of people walk by.

I hear the crunch as my eyes slam shut.

Fuck. Fuck. Fuck.

"Aw, shit," someone grumbles. I straighten and look down at where my smashed phone is being scooped up by big, meaty hands.

"Shit, man, I'm sorry. I saw it right as it was too late." The massive dude hands me my phone. The screen is shattered six ways from Sunday. I tap at the screen and nothing happens.

"Really, man. I'm sorry," he offers. Pressing my lips tight, I just nod, not bothering to look at him. My lack of response must piss him off because he doesn't shut up. "Maybe don't leave your phone on the floor in a busy walkway next time."

Whipping my head toward him, I glare daggers. I open my mouth to rip him a new one when Simon steps up.

"All right, advice noted." He shoves me a little in the opposite direction of the beefy man and his friends. I glare at him for a second longer as I let Simon steer me away before I can say something shitty back.

"I'm sure you can find time to stop by an Apple store before we head home," Simon says by my side.

I just stare down at my phone, pissed at my fucking luck.

FOURTEEN

Kelly

Leaning over the granite counter, I mindlessly tap the pen between my fingers on the application I'm supposed to be reviewing.

Another puppy finding its forever home. It's bittersweet, sending these little furballs home. It's so easy to become attached to them, but I'm always so happy when they finally find their forever family.

Normally, I don't work weekends, but I had nothing better to do today, so I came in anyway. Off the clock. That should be a testament to how much I really enjoy my job—that I'm willing to work without pay. Letting out a sigh, I try to refocus my attention.

"Well, that doesn't sound good," a voice behind me sings. Looking over my shoulder, I give Aubrey a tired smile.

"What are you doing here?" I ask.

She snorts. "I should ask you the same."

"We had an abundance of applications come in the past couple of days. I wanted to go through them before Monday." I tap the sheet I'm holding with the pen again.

"Okay, but you could do that at home. Instead, you're here. In my shelter. Bringing down the vibe." She leans her hip against the counter, arms crossed over her chest, and she's giving me a look that says, *Don't argue, you know I'm right.*

"You kicking me out?" I ask, my brow furrowing.

"Nope, but now I'm asking what's up with you. You've been mopey, which is not your default setting."

"Just having a bad week." I scoop up the applications and stuff them in a file folder. I suppose I could watch some *New Girl* while I review these. I need a healthy dose of Nick Miller.

"Uh-huh," is all she says as she follows me back toward the office.

"You wanna talk about it, cupcake?"

I smile at the nickname. "Not particularly."

"Do you *need* to talk about it?" she counters.

I snag my purse off the desk in the back office and heave a sigh. "Probably."

"All right. Lucky for you, I'm heading home, too. So you and I are gonna get some wine and order in some tacos."

"Is it even two yet?" I question as she flips the light in the office off.

"Does it matter?" she quips.

"Where's Chance tonight?"

"He's helping his sister with some shelving. So if we play our cards right, he'll bring home milkshakes after tacos."

Hmmm. I chuckle. "So wine, tacos, and milkshakes are your answers to a bad week?"

"It's what my girl loves, so, yeah. We can do shots instead of wine if you want."

"Maybe milkshakes and tacos, then wine later," I offer. Not sure I can handle wine before milkshakes.

"Anything you want, boo." She wraps her arm around me and squeezes me tight.

Thirty minutes later, we sit at the picnic table near the beach with tacos and milkshakes.

"All right, spill it." She wraps up a shrimp taco.

"Ben and I... Well, I think we're over," I say sadly, looking down at my fish taco. It's one of my favorite things ever, and I can't even enjoy it. My appetite is suddenly nonexistent.

"What? Really?" Aubrey sets down her own taco.

"Yeah. I mean, I haven't heard from him in a week. So..."

Her eyes bulge. "He's not dead, is he?" She slaps her hand over her mouth. "Shit."

"I mean, I don't think so. He's at a convention. I peeked at his Twitter feed. He's been tweeting."

"Have your texts and calls gone unanswered?" she asks quietly.

"Pretty much. My last text went unanswered. I called yesterday, too. Nothing." I finally take a bite. I chew slowly, thinking about this hole I've found myself in.

She reaches over and places her hand on my arm. "You didn't say much about your trip to Chicago, but that's when I noticed the sadness. Did something happen in Chicago?"

I scrunch my face and recall that weekend two weeks ago. What a freaking roller coaster ride that trip was. "The visit started out amazing. He was engaged and extremely happy to see me."

She waggles her eyebrow. "Like, really happy?"

I snort. "Yeah, we couldn't keep our hands off each

other. But on the second day, he got a phone call about a job, and things went downhill from there."

"A job? Is he in the market?"

"Yeah, he's going to retire from the team soon. He's been thinking about his next step for a while." I wave that off and continue to tell her about the weekend. "Anyway, he was withdrawn and snippy. He didn't want to tell me about the call or the job when I asked. By the time he dropped me off at the airport, it was like he couldn't get away from me quick enough. He said he had a lot of shit to figure out, whatever that means. That he needed space to figure it out."

"I don't think you could give him any more space," she mutters.

"I know, right? But he hugged me and said he was sorry and told me to text when I got home." I shrugged.

"Okay." She says slowly. "So are things still rocky?"

"Well, we still text every day, but the calls have become few and far between. There have been times where we text throughout the whole day, but in the past week, our communication has been nothing more than a random text here and there."

She curses under her breath, but I don't miss the string of nasty words.

"All right. What's going through your head right now?" She chews on her lip.

"I'm thinking that I was falling really freaking hard for him. So much so I was considering what would happen if I moved to Chicago at some point." Aubrey's eyes nearly pop out of her head as I continue. "But now... now I'm thinking I might have just set a record of the shortest relationship I've ever had." I place my cheek into my palm, my elbow leaning on the rough wood table.

She sighs. "Oh, Kelly."

Squeezing my eyes shut, I fight back the tears.

"You think you two are through without even officially ending it?" Her voice is soft, laced with concern.

I just nod, my eyes still closed. She sighs, but it's quiet for a few beats.

"Well, I think it's bullshit," she seethes.

My eyes pop open and take her in. She looks downright pissed. "I liked the guy. I really did. I saw the way you looked at him, and the way he looked at you. This connection between you runs deep, even if it's young. But long-distance relationships are hard. You gotta fight for what you want."

"But what if what I want isn't worth fighting for?" A tear springs free. "What if I don't want a long-distance relationship? I knew it was a bad idea, I just didn't want to lose him so quickly. But it's not what I want. I want Ben, but not if he doesn't want me. And honestly, after the way he's acted over the past two weeks, I think he's made his intentions clear."

She shakes her head, opens her mouth, then shuts it. I gaze off at the ocean, wishing I could be out there without a care in the world.

"Then I think you need to be the one to end it. No more of this "I think it's over" crap. Call him, text him, email him—hell, fly out there and end it face to face. He doesn't deserve your tears. But you deserve to put this behind you and move on."

I never take my eyes off the horizon, but I nod in acknowledgment. I know she's right. I deserve more. Better. She lets me wallow for a bit longer, then we head home. She pours us wine and then we pop in my favorite movie, *Pitch Perfect*.

We drink wine before switching to shots. I know, I

know. *Wine before liquor, never sicker.* But when you're heartbroken, you make stupid decisions.

The room is spinning as I tumble into my bed. I shove one foot over the side of the bed and plant it firmly on the ground. I take deep breaths in and out as I start to calm the storm that's sure to be a gnarly hangover. Suddenly, I contemplate calling Ben. I think it through for all of about five seconds before I'm slapping around on my bed for my discarded phone. I can't open my eyes to pull up his number, so I say, "Siri, callllll Ven." But my words are slurred so my British male Siri replies, "Did you mean Ben from your contacts?"

"Yessss," I gripe.

"Calling Ben," he replies.

Ring after ring, there's no answer. His voicemail starts rolling, and while I shouldn't leave a message, I think about what I should say. The beep sounds and I say nothing. I'm at a loss for words and then I hear an automated voice say, "Goodbye." And the line goes dead.

Silently, I curse him for breaking my heart just like I expected he would.

I don't leave a message, but I lie there, staring at the ceiling and wondering how I got here. Fine, if he won't answer, I'll text him. I open my eyes, worried about the room spinning again, but nothing moves so I place the phone up in my face and type. Slowly, though—the keyboard is blurry.

ME: I can't do this anymore.
   Me: We're done.

. . .

MINUTES, I think—maybe longer—go by before I pry open one eye to see if he responded. Disappointment and fury seethe through me. There's no answer. I don't know why I expected him to break his silence now. Anger fuses through my bones, wrapping its way around my heart and nearly strangling me. I text Ben one final time.

ME: You're a fucking asshole.

I'M TOO mad and too drunk to cry. I did enough of that this afternoon when I told my best friend everything. So, no, I don't cry. But waves of nausea roll through me. Shooting up in bed, I push myself off the bed and stumble through the room and into the small bathroom. Leaning over the toilet, I start praying to the porcelain god that I will never, ever drink again.

Tears roll down my cheeks—it's just par for the course when I get sick. They aren't tears for Ben.

No.

Fuck Ben Ford and his stupid face.

And fuck you, fate, for putting him in my path so many times.

"Universe, go fuck yourself," I growl, gritting my teeth before another coil of acid comes roaring up my throat.

At some point, I make it back to my bed. Late twenties is far too old to be spending the night next to the toilet. Eventually, I roll out of my bed and walk, eyes closed, through my tiny apartment. My hands out in front of me, I fumble around as I walk to the kitchen to find Advil and pour a glass of water. After shooting down the meds, I slowly make my way to the bathroom, brush my teeth, and swish around some mouthwash. I know I reek, and I plan on a shower as soon as the medicine starts working.

I face plant into the couch and groan as I realize it's way too bright in here. I contemplate moving back to my room when there's a knock at the door.

"Go away," I mumble.

The knock comes again, and I grumble into the couch.

"Kelly, you dead in there?" I recognize Chance's voice and groan as I draw myself up. As I go, I grab the sunglasses that sit on the coffee table, shoving them on before I unlock the door.

Squinting and covering my face, I hiss as if I'm a vampire seeing the sun. Shit, I feel like I'm dying, that's for sure.

Chance's deep chuckle doesn't help. "Shit, Kelly. You've seen better days, my friend."

I leave the door open and walk back to the couch, smashing my face into the cushion. I hear him chuckle again and then the door quietly shuts. After seeing the sun, the room isn't nearly as bright as I thought.

"What do you want?" I groan.

"I figured since Aubrey just crawled into bed after spending half the night in the bathroom, you probably would be in a similar situation. My suspicions weren't wrong. You need a shower, kid. You stink."

"I'm not dead. And I'll shower as soon as the medicine I just took kicks in."

"You're grumbly. And it's fun." And he's a jerk. His voice is light, but he's not speaking very loud so at least he's a considerate jerk.

"What do you want?" I whine again.

"I brought coffee." My ears perk up at his words. It's like lifting a hundred pounds, but I manage to lift my head off the couch.

"Really?"

"Yup. But ya gotta sit up to drink it."

I do just as he suggests. It takes effort, but I do it. He hands me the coffee, and that's when I see he has a yellow-wrapped breakfast sandwich for me.

"I didn't know your preference, but Aubrey loves the sausage biscuits, so I got you one, too." He hands it over. The iconic greasy breakfast sandwich smell hits my nose, and I nearly sigh with content.

"Egg and cheese, too?" I whimper as I unwrap it.

"Only the best for my hungover wife and her best friend." He takes a seat in the one recliner next to the couch as I take a bite.

Through a moan, I tell him, "Thank you." He lets me get a few more bites in before talking again.

He clears his throat. "So. Last night. You were really feeling the booze."

"Bad week." A take a sip of coffee.

"Yeah, I heard."

I make eye contact with him as I chew, and I can tell he wants to say more. "Spit it out." I don't care if I still have food in my mouth.

"Aubrey and I don't like seeing you like this. Do you need me to help with anything?" Sometimes I forget he's from Australia, his accent only coming out occasionally.

My face softens. He's such a good man. "Thank you," I tell him. My phone pings at my side, and I pull it out of the hoodie pocket, totally forgetting I shoved it in there as I was rolling out of bed.

AUBREY: Are you alive? I sent Chance to save you if you are indeed dead.

. . .

SNORTING, I type back.

Me: Not dead anymore. The sandwich and coffee were a good call.

"IS THAT MY WIFE?" he asks as I look down at my phone. I tell him yeah as I leave her text thread and see my most recent texts.

Oh, shit. The last words I texted last night are all I see.

"What's wrong, Kelly?" Chance's voice is laced with concern.

"Oh, no. Oh, no. Oh, no," I mutter and tears fill my eyes, my vision blurring.

"Kelly," he growls. I read aloud the last three messages I sent Ben. I close my eyes and lean my head back against the couch.

"Tell me what's wrong," he bites out.

"Apparently, in my drunken state, I texted Ben." I cover my eyes, remembering I still have sunglasses on. I yank them off and wipe my eyes.

"Oh. Well, I mean, did you initiate some sexy texts or something?" He doesn't sound concerned anymore.

"Worse. I broke up with him and called him a fucking asshole." My words wobble on the last part.

Chance just whistles.

"Yeah." I squeeze my eyes shut and take a deep breath. Chance is quiet beside me. "I could use that help now."

He coughs. "In what way?"

"Advice. I need to know how to fix this." I wave my cell phone over my lap. He doesn't say anything, so I peek my eye open and look at him. He's looking at me pensively.

"What?"

"Does this need fixing, Kel? Were you just telling

Aubrey last night that it was over between you two? Maybe," he leans forward, "you should just leave it be."

I shake my head. "No, this can't be the last thing I say to him. We deserve more than a breakup over text."

"Call him," he offers.

"He doesn't answer."

He studies me for a moment. "Then go to him. Make him listen."

My mouth hangs open. "You mean…" I swallow. "You mean, I should fly out to Chicago just to apologize and break up with him face to face?"

"You deserve that closure, don't you?" He tilts his head.

I chew on the inside of my cheek.

"What would you do?" I finally ask, looking up at him while his eyes glitter.

"What I *did* was fight for what I wanted."

I take in his words. I know his and Aubrey's story. The very long path the two of them wandered down in order to find their happily ever after.

"I just don't know that what we have would work in the long run. I think he's checked out," I whisper.

"Maybe. And if that's the case, then he isn't worth it. But maybe it's not, and maybe you need to find out the truth." We stare at each other. He grins the longer I glare.

"Gah." I throw my hands up in the air. He cocks his head. "I have to ask my boss for a couple of days off."

He laughs. "I think it will be approved." He stands and walks to the door. "I'd take a shower before you leave, though."

I roll my eyes, but as he has one foot out of my door, I yell, "Thanks, Chance."

Looking over his shoulder, he tells me, "Anytime, Kel. Anytime."

FIFTEEN

Ben

It's our last day at E3, and while the week is always so crazy hectic, it's still worth it to attend. We get to meet fans, catch up with industry friends, and make new contacts. But sleep sounds so fucking good at this point that the countdown to head home is almost as exciting as the final day of events. We're all boarding a flight this afternoon, but something's gnawing away at me.

Not something—someone.

Kelly.

I know I've been a major dick not contacting her as much. But I'm in California, and it feels wrong of me to not see Kelly.

Actually, it makes me feel like utter shit. I should go see her.

I'm sitting on the floor, leaning against the wall of our tiny meeting room. Without a phone, I can't spend my downtime checking emails or mindlessly scrolling through Twitter. My last tweet was a couple of days ago, actually—a few minutes before my phone died its very quick, yet painful death.

Thanks to our contacts, one of Team NoMad's sponsors was able to secure me a loner phone. Problem was, it wasn't a smart phone, and since I have an iPhone, I couldn't access my contacts. I didn't realize how much of my life was on my phone until now. I miss my fucking phone, that's for sure. I sit here, flipping through a pile of marketing materials that were in the swag bag from the presentation I just attended. Bernie wanders into the room. Seeing me, she smiles. I nod at her, and she walks over and slides down against the wall to join me.

"Hey, Simon just mentioned you were on our flight. Are you not going to see Kelly?" She frowns.

Well, speak of the devil.

"Uh, no, I wasn't going to." I rub my jaw.

"Okay." She draws out the word. "Why is that?"

"Things aren't great between us right now."

"How so?"

I sigh, not wanting to get into this right now. But I know she won't back down at this point. "I told her I needed some space to figure out things. And, well, things have been strained since she left Chicago."

Her forehead creases in worry. "What?"

"I need to figure out what's next for me, and I need to do that without a girlfriend who lives thousands of miles away making me feel bad for moving even further." I cock my eyebrow at her, hoping she gets it.

Realization dawns on her. "Oh, you mean that job with Gallant?"

"How do you know about it?" I ask.

"You know Simon is just as much of a gossip as Link and Dex. Nothing is safe." She laughs. It's true. I should have guessed that if one of them knew, they would all know. I'm going to have to tell them I'm leaving sooner than later. Or I'll end up with a going away party before I even know I'm going away. I roll my eyes as I lean my head against the wall.

"I thought you and Kelly were serious," she questions. "Well, as serious as you can be in a long-distance relationship."

"Ahh. Yeah, see, I think we're getting too serious too fast. And, well, it didn't feel right to me to include her in such a big life decision when we were so new." I close my eyes, internally cursing myself as I realize I've been an utter dick.

"That's a dick move," she mumbles.

"So I've been told," I say plainly. I take a moment to conjure Kelly in my mind. Her thick brown hair, the seawater causing her luscious tendrils to twist and curve into waves. Her soft face and sinful lips. I want to reach out to her, pull her into me, and breathe her deep into my lungs. I love how she always smells of the beach and sunny weather. My vision of Kelly fades away when Bernie replies.

"I think when you find the one, you just know. And whether you've been with someone for a month or years, when you've got a life change coming on, you include the other person since it will affect them, too."

I can feel her staring at my profile, but I don't open my eyes yet. So, she continues, "Moving to New York would have affected your relationship. She should have an opportunity to share her opinion on it."

I grunt.

She's quiet for a moment, before asking, "How have things been strained?"

That when I look at her. I know she sees the guilt because it's nearly drowning me. "I stopped texting and calling."

Her mouth drops open.

"Not completely," I rush to add. "Before, we were texting and calling every day. And, well, I just tried to back off a bit."

She shakes her head, not even attempting to hide the disgusted look on her face.

"I thought you were on my side," I grumble.

"While I'm your friend and will always have your back, unfortunately, I'm on the side of girl code at the moment. You did her wrong, Ben. It's time you realize it."

My shoulders drop. "I do realize it."

"Then change your flight and go to Hermosa Beach tonight and apologize. Things between you two might not work out, but maybe they will. Either way, you owe her a massive apology and the truth about what's going on."

I hang my head. The flight change is gonna cost me, but I think Bernie is right—I owe Kelly a big fucking apology.

"Okay. You're right," I mutter into my chest.

"I should have recorded that. Would you say it again in just a moment?" She leans toward me to yank her phone out of her pocket.

I chuckle. "Not a chance."

She pushes her bottom lip out in a mock pout.

I pat around on the floor looking for my phone before I remember it's back in my hotel room, still shattered. "Hey, since I don't have a new phone yet, and I can't do anything useful on this loaner, can I use your phone to change my flights?"

"I can't believe that happened to your phone." She shakes her head in disbelief but hands me her phone.

With a tiny bit of hope and a renewed sense of purpose, I quickly change my flight. All that matters now is that I'm doing something I should have done days ago.

A few hours later, my team departs for LAX, and I grab a cab for the forty-five minute ride to Hermosa.

Not gonna lie, not having a phone for the past two days hasn't been horrible. However, I don't love just showing up at Kelly's door unexpectedly. A pang of worry hits me hard when I realize that, even if she texted me in the past two days, I wouldn't have replied, making the time since we've talked even longer.

Shit.

I hope she doesn't think I'm dead. However, I'm probably a dead man anyway.

I spend the ride thinking of all the ways she's going to tell me she hates me. I really fucked this up. I got in my head and didn't let her in, and I have this deep down, gut feeling I've screwed things up between us. If I were her, I'd drop me hard and quick. But because I'm not her—I'm me—I hope she gives me another chance.

Unfortunately, without my phone, I don't remember Kelly's address. Which is something I don't realize until we arrive in Hermosa Beach. But I remember the name of the Animal Shelter she works at, so I tell him where I need to go.

I remember that the shelter is within walking distance to her place, so I'll check with the shelter on the off chance they'll tell me where she lives. If not, maybe they'll call her for me.

When the cab drives off, I turn and see a woman locking up the front door of the shelter. I try not to rush her, but I don't want to have to chase her down.

"Ma'am," I yell out to her. She whips around, and I let out a breath. I recognize her. Kelly introduced us when she brought me to the shelter last time I was here.

"Hi." She smiles, and I can tell she's trying to place my face.

"I'm Ben, Kelly's boyfriend from Chicago. We met several weeks ago." I smile too, trying not to let on that I'm stressed she might not remember me. But her face lights up.

"Oh, yeah, the gamer. I remember!" She steps away from the building, and that's when I notice the hours on the window. The shelter's closed for the night which means Kelly isn't here. But that makes sense because she doesn't work on Sundays. So, here goes nothing.

"Long story short, I came to surprise Kelly. I realized as we entered Hermosa that I don't have her address. But I remembered the shelter. I know I can walk to her place from here, but could you give me directions?" I send a silent thought to the big man upstairs that she doesn't flip out and withhold the info I so desperately need.

She smiles—I dig through my mind for her name—and nods. "Yeah, of course. She's going to be so excited to see you!" Then she rattles off how to get to Kelly's apartment. Remembering her name is Amanda, I thank her profusely before heading that way.

The directions were pretty easy, and it's only a fifteen-minute walk, but by the time her over-the-garage apartment comes into view, I'm done with dragging my suitcase behind me.

I climb the rickety stairs and finally set down my suitcase. I'm pretty sure one of the wheels is about to pop off. I knock, and there's nothing. I knock again, and I still don't hear anything from inside the apartment.

She must not be home. Sighing, I pick up my suitcase and head back down the stairs. I guess my next stop is next door.

This time when I knock, the door swings open. Aubrey's big smile fades to a frown faster than you can say, *I'm indeed a fucking dead man.*

"What the hell?" she growls.

"Hi, Aubrey. I'm looking for Kelly." Being sweet is not my forte, but damn, I clearly have to tread lightly with her.

"Yeah, she isn't here." She crosses her arms.

"I figured. I just tried her door." I point toward the garage. "I was hoping you knew where she was."

She glares at me. "Maybe try calling her. Or texting her. Or I don't know, *communicating* with her in any form."

Lifting my hand to the back of my neck, I hang my head a bit. "You probably won't believe me, but my phone got destroyed. So I don't have her number at the moment. Once I got to Hermosa, I realized I didn't know her address off the top of my head either. I had the cab drop me off at the shelter, then asked Amanda as she was locking up for directions to Kelly's. Fortunately, she could help me out."

Aubrey's eyes bulge. "We don't make it a habit of giving out personal information."

"It's not lost on me how incredibly lucky I am she recognized me." I shove my hands in my pockets. "So, do you know when Kelly will be back?"

Aubrey laughs then, and it's not a fun, happy laugh. It's actually kind of scary. "Kelly went to Chicago."

Her words slam into me like a herd of fucking elephants. Aubrey reads the room and visibly loses her hold on her anger.

"She decided since she couldn't get ahold of you, she needed a face-to-face. She's probably landing soon—if she hasn't already." She leans against the doorjamb, watching me closely.

"Can you call her? Tell her I'm here?" My voice is strained. Her nose scrunches, then she sighs.

"Fine," she says, bringing her phone to her ear. She doesn't answer, so she leaves a message.

"Hey, Kel, you need to call me back ASAP. You won't believe what the cat dragged in." She hangs up. Trying not to be annoyed that the message she left doesn't help me at all, I force my grin and thank her.

"What are you going to do now?" she snaps.

"I'm going to stick around until I hear back from her." I eye the comfy-looking porch set to the left of Aubrey's front door. No way she lets me relax here. She's gonna make me wait on the old metal steps at the garage. "Is there an AT&T around here? I need to get a new phone as soon as possible."

She studies me and then relents. "Yeah, it's a few blocks. Maybe a twenty-minute walk in the opposite direction you just came." She points down the street and gives me simple instructions. I ask her if I can leave my suitcase on her porch and she, thankfully, tells me yes.

As collateral, I leave my suitcase next to Aubrey's front door and hope to God the store is still open at four o'clock on a Sunday.

It was.

An hour later, I make my way back to Kelly's. With my new phone, I call her. No answer, so I text her. No answer.

She's either still in the air or giving me a taste of my own medicine. I remember I left my suitcase on Aubrey's porch, but I wasn't invited to hang out on her comfy porch chair. So, I wander over to the stairs leading up to Kelly's apartment.

Taking a seat on the second step, I focus on my phone, downloading my favorite apps, and checking my email. Basically, doing anything to pass the time while I wait to hear back from Kelly. I shift a few times as my ass goes numb. I'm gonna have to bite the bullet and ask Aubrey if I can sit on her chair.

Forty-five minutes go by before I hear the front door of

the house next door open. Turning my head, I see Chance walk out, close the door behind him, and jog down the stairs. His walk is casual, non-threatening, so I don't get the feeling he's about to make this situation awkward. Hopefully he isn't about to rip into me like I know his wife wants to do.

"Yo." He nods, his hands in the front pockets of his jeans.

"Hey." I drop my hands between my knees, breaking my contact with my phone.

"You've been out here for a while, eh?"

"Yeah, I'll wait until I hear from Kelly." I tread carefully. I know this is his property, and that Kelly rents from them, so technically he can kick me off it.

"Good. I heard you've been without a phone." His eyebrow raises.

I snort. "Yeah. I dropped it at the exact wrong time because some guy stepped right on it."

He cringes. "Ouch."

"Yeah."

"So new phone then." He gestures to my hand.

"As of about an hour ago."

"You back your shit up to the cloud?" He shoves his hand back into his pocket. It's a strange conversation, but I go with it.

"Call me cheap, but I don't pay for cloud space. I only back up data I can't lose. Contacts, mainly. Everything else, meh..." I unhurriedly lift my shoulder.

He nods like he agrees. "I don't back up my texts."

"Me neither," I offer. He visibly relaxes. "Why?"

"No biggie, mate. It's just that sometimes women get drunk and say shit they don't mean. Now, you can't hold it against her. She'll be relieved to find out her text will remain unseen."

Ahh. Now I'm curious what my sweet, fun-loving Kelly could have said while drunk.

I lift an eyebrow. "That bad?"

He chortles. "Not as bad as the words my wife has been using when referring to you."

I groan. If I can convince Kelly to give me a second chance, I'm gonna have my work cut out for me to get back into her good graces.

Chance wears a massive grin as he beckons to me, turning on his heel. "Come on, no need to sit out on the rickety old stoop. Come inside and sit on the couch. I'll get you something to drink. You can play with Pixy."

"Your wife all right with this?" I ask as I stand, stretching out my back. I'm still unable to feel my ass.

He bellows out a laugh. "Who do you think sent me?"

"I thought maybe you went rogue or something. Bro code, maybe," I mutter as I follow behind him toward his house.

"Well, I may have done a little sweet-talking on your behalf. But you sitting out here, sticking around, helped."

It's my turn to laugh. Maybe it won't take too much to get Aubrey back on my side. That is, after I talk to Kelly, see where she is in terms of our relationship, then work my numb ass off to get her to give me another chance.

SIXTEEN

Kelly

I'm one of those people that hate to ask others for their address or phone number twice. I write shit down. So, as I open up the door of Ben's apartment building, I'm grateful for my obsessive habit. I added his address to his contact info in my phone the moment we arrived from the airport a few weeks ago.

I take a moment to reacquaint myself with the lobby. Ben lives in a high-rise that has a front desk, security, and a handful of other amenities most apartments don't. I've never asked Ben how much he makes, but he's got to make good money to be able to afford this place. There are large leather couches and a fireplace to one side, elevators to the back, and the front desk has two older gentlemen standing behind. They eye me, but I smile and pretend I'm not utterly exhausted and still slightly hungover.

I know I probably look like shit, but whatever. I look how I feel.

"Hi. My name is Kelly Spencer. I'm here to see Ben Ford." I lean against the tall granite counter. The man smiles at me while he types in my name. I assume to see if I'm on the list.

"Looks like you are on the list, but Mr. Ford..." he trails off just as I hear a familiar voice.

"Kelly?" I turn my head toward the elevators and see Bernie, along with the rest of Ben's teammates, waiting for the doors to open. All of them are laden with suitcases and backpacks. They're clearly coming and not going.

"Hey, Bernie." I wave, searching for Ben. He's not with the group, but I recognize Dex, Simon, Link and his girlfriend, Ruby. Bernie waves the group on just as the elevator doors slide open. She rushes toward me.

"Hey, Ralph, she's good. I'll take her up." She smiles at him and nods toward the elevator.

"Thank you," I tell her, but she frowns.

"What are you doing here, Kelly?" I stumble a moment, unsure of why her question concerns me.

"Uh, to see Ben."

Her eyes widen. "He's not here in Chicago. He's still in California."

I come to a dead stop. "What do you mean in California?"

Pity. All I see is pity in her eyes, and my blood starts to boil.

"We've all been in LA for the past several days. We all just got back from dinner. But Ben decided to stay and visit you." I drink in her words, and her mouth tightens. "So you're here and he's there. Oh. My. God."

"Why wouldn't he tell me? Call or text?" My words come out soft despite the raging anger threatening to take over.

"His phone was crushed. It's unusable. He was going to get a new one today." She pauses as the elevator door slides open. I look to it, then to her, wondering if I should just leave. I should just go back to the airport and catch a flight. I don't know why, but I never booked a flight home. I didn't know what to expect when I arrived in Chicago. But Bernie seems to have other plans for me. She walks a few steps toward me and grabs my hand. "Come on up. Let's get this figured out," she says, pulling me toward the elevator.

Stepping on after her, I shake my head. "I don't understand."

"You haven't heard from him?" she asks, like she's trying to defuse a hostile situation.

"No, nothing." I pull out my phone from my bag and realize it's still shut off from the flight. I power it up, and as we step out of the elevator, I'm hit with a bunch of messages. Both texts and voicemails. I study the notifications on the lock screen.

AUBREY: What the hell, Kel? Call me!!!
Aubrey: Chance is making me play nice.
Ben: I can't feel my ass anymore. Where are you?
Ben: I'll wait on your step until I hear from you.
Aubrey: You won't believe what the cat dragged in.

THEY CONTINUE, but I swipe open my phone and call Aubrey first. Bernie wanders deep into her apartment before flipping on the first light, illuminating the darkness. I follow her inside just as the call connects.

"Bout time, girlfriend," Aubrey rushes.

I drop my bag by the front door and watch Bernie turn on lights and make her way into her apartment. "What's going on? Ben is there?" I ask.

"Uh, yeah. He showed up like two hours ago." She

lowers her voice. "I don't know what to do with him. He looks like a sad puppy. It's making it hard for me to stay mad at him."

I grunt and roll my eyes. Not about her feeling bad, but that he has the audacity to be sad. "He never told me he was in California. And how he's there, and I'm here."

"Ironic, yeah?" She huffs out a laugh. "Where are you?"

"I'm with Bernie, his friend. She lives in the same building." Bernie points to the couch, and I wander through the small space and sit down.

"Okay, so what's the plan?" Aubrey asks.

"I guess one of us needs to leave," I mumble. I suck in the corner of my lip, thinking things through. "I'll head back to the airport and get the next flight out."

"Okay. So it's gonna be a late night then," she huffs.

"Just let him into my apartment, and I'll text you when I'm home so you don't have to worry. You also won't have to deal with any of my drama."

"Your drama is my drama. It's not a big deal. I'm just still feeling last night. Maybe we should cool it on the rage drinking from now on."

A laugh slips out and I nod, even though she can't see me. "Agreed."

I wait a beat. "So he's there right now?"

"Yeah. Watching some game with Chance—who's totally Team Ben by the way. I mean, he's made it clear to me he's always got your back, but don't be surprised if he tries to build a case for Ben. Just fair warning.

I sigh. It doesn't surprise me.

"Do you want to talk to him?" she whispers.

"Chance? No," I absentmindedly reply.

A snort comes over the phone. "No, Ben. He's staring me down right now."

Do I want to talk to him?

Absofuckinglutly.

But, I won't. I'm mad and need to time process what the heck just happened.

"I'll let you guys know my flight info. See you later." We say our goodbyes and then I use Bernie's laptop to book my flight.

I got a hell of a deal on a last-minute flight, but what surprises me is that after walking me down to my waiting Uber, Bernie climbs in next to me.

"What are you doing?"

"Riding with you." She shrugs as if I should expect nothing less. "Also, I wanted to talk to you. About Ben."

Sighing, I buckle up. "Bernie, I don't know what's going on. I have to fly home first to figure it out."

"I know, but since you have to wait a few more hours to get that explanation, I'm going to get involved. Because, well, I care about you both."

I nod, letting her know I'm not going to stop her.

"Things get really, really busy for us this time of year."

"Don't make excuses," I deadpan.

"I'm not." Her pause is short. "Okay, I am. But I'll stop."

"I'm not asking him to visit me. To make time for me. I'm asking for him to return texts. Maybe a call or two. And for fuck's sake, to tell me when he's less than an hour drive away from where I live."

It's dark out, but the night lights still show all the sadness in her eyes when she looks at me and nods.

"I know." Her voice soft.

"It's that job, isn't it? He had an offer, but he won't share anything about it." I turn toward her. I know it's that job that mucked everything up between us. I just wish he would have been open with me about it.

"That's something he has to explain. But I will say it's been causing him a lot of heart and headache. The next step—leaving what you know—it's a hard step to take."

Without thinking, I snap at her, "Well, it's something you normally talk to your significant other about. Instead, he shut me the fuck out."

She shakes her head, but she surprises me again. "No, Kelly, I know. I agree with you. He didn't handle it well, and I'm sorry for that." Her agreement helps simmer my anger. Then she adds, "You might not know this, but Ben doesn't like relying on other people. He's not a loner, but he's alone a lot. The team is important to him, and we consider him a friend, but he doesn't easily let people in. He makes decisions on his own. He likes to make them before he lets anyone else know about them. It's annoying as hell, but it's who he is. He's got some stuff he needs to work through, but don't give up on him. Please." Her voice is pleading.

I lean my head back onto the car seat and close my eyes. "I'm not sure if it's a matter of giving up, or just facing the music. Long-distance relationships suck, and if one half of the couple isn't able to remain open and honest, then, well…" I don't finish the sentence.

We sit in silence for several minutes, then Bernie tries to make small talk. I appreciate her. And I tell her that as I pull her into an embrace when the Uber drops me off at the airport.

I find my way to the terminal and take a seat on one of the benches. This late at night, I'm surprised at how many are waiting to board along with me.

I huff, noting the time—it's nearly nine. I want to curl up and sleep this freaking day away and not think about it again.

Knowing Ben's at my place, I start to get antsy. While I wait to board, I pull out my phone and text him.

ME: How's the ass?

UNLIKE OVER THE past two weeks, his response is immediate.

BEN: Better.
Me: Good.
Ben: Aubrey hates me, but this goat is my new best friend.
Me: Pixy loves everyone.
Ben: Don't take this away from me. I've never had a goat friend before.

I LET a few moments go by before responding.

ME: What the hell happened, Ben?
Ben: I fucked up. I'm so sorry, baby.

HE'S NEVER CALLED me baby before. I'm equally annoyed and relieved that he's started now. But I leave it at a simple *okay* since it's time for me to get on the plane. He'll have plenty of time to explain and apologize in person—at, like, three in the morning when I arrive home. You bet your ass I'm not going to let this wait another second. We'll figure this shit out once and for all.

SEVENTEEN

Kelly

I'd be happy if I don't see the inside of an airplane any time soon. I'm not a huge fan of flying, and doing it by myself, even less. The fact that I've been on a plane four times in three weeks sucks donkey balls and I'm over it. When the Uber drops me off in front of Aubrey and Chance's house, it's a little after one. It's going to take me a hot minute to get my body back into the right time zone. Due to the three-hour time change, this day has definitely been the longest day of my life. And I'm nearly dead on my feet.

Standing on the sidewalk, I send Aubrey a quick text to let her know I'm home—as promised. When I glance at my apartment, I can tell there's a light on. I take a deep breath, knowing he's awake and we can't wait to work through our shit until I've had a nap.

I ready myself with another deep breath and a small pep talk as I make my way to the stairs. I attempt to be quiet as I ascend the stairs, but they creak with every step.

I unlock my door and slowly open it. The light in the kitchen is on, but the rest of the room is dark. That's when

I see him—he's stretched out on my couch. He doesn't move, so he must be asleep. Why wouldn't he sleep in my bed? I never made him sleep on the couch when he visited.

I gently close the door behind me, locking it before I drop my bag on the floor. I deposit my purse on the small table next to the door, dropping my keys there as well.

Do I wake him? I want to sleep so badly, but he's here, in my space, and I don't want to waste a minute of that time. I'm so angry with him, but my heart begs me to go to him. My fingers itch to touch him. My body is drawn to him. The only thing keeping me rooted in place is my brain telling me to wait. At least I can trust one part of myself.

I take him in. Jeans, signature black tee. He's wearing a beanie, though, something I've not seen him wear before. He's got the hat pulled down, possibly covering his eyes. His arms are crossed over his chest, his chin tucked in close. I can tell he started propped up in the corner, one leg stretched out across the couch, the other bent, foot planted on the floor. He still dons his black and white chucks.

I would love nothing more than to go to him, crawl over him, and snuggle into his side. Would he have me or would he want to talk instead? The battle between my heart and head comes to an end when my feet move toward the couch. I kneel on the floor and slowly reach for his beanie.

Lifting it up, I whisper, "Ben."

His eyes blink open as he takes me in. He's not startled. Then a lazy grin crosses his face, and the need to kiss him settles deep in my belly. I fight it, though. There will be no kissing until we figure things out.

"Kel." His voice is hoarse. He clears it, shaking his head slightly.

"Hey." I drop my hand from him as he sits up.

"What time is it?" he asks, his deep voice back to normal.

"Just after one." Suddenly there isn't much space between us, so I lean back on my haunches. He tugs off his beanie, and it takes everything in me not to gasp in surprise. His messy, thick, finger-tangling hair is gone.

"Your hair," I murmur.

His hand comes up and scrubs over his new buzz cut. "Oh, yeah, I needed a change." When he peers at me, his eyes are filled with worry. "Do you hate it?"

I cock my head and take him in. While I loved running my fingers through his hair, this new style suits him just as much as the pompadour did. It makes his bad boy vibe more pronounced.

"I do. I just wasn't expecting it," I tell him.

"Okay, good." He gives me a shy smile—one I've never seen before.

Awkwardness takes over and it's nearly excruciating. Never once when we've seen each other after weeks between visits—even before we started dating—was it this awkward. We always just picked up where we left off.

I huff and push up on my feet. Standing, I look down at him. "I've gotta change and brush my teeth." I walk to my bag, snag it up, and carry it toward my room. I hear him get up from the couch, and he follows a safe distance behind. Tossing my bag on the bed, I pull out a pair of sleep shorts and a tank, a clean pair of undies, and my toiletry bag. He leans against the doorjamb, watching me. Under different circumstances, I'd just change right here in front of him. I'm not shy, but you can cut the tension between us with a butter knife. Besides, why should I treat him to a show? I'm pissed at him.

So, I grab my stuff and book it to my bathroom. He doesn't say a word as I change and brush the day-old sweaters off my teeth. When I return to my room, he's sitting on my bed, his shoes on the floor where I stood moments ago.

Making eye contact, he starts to open his mouth, but I beat him to the punch. "Why are you here, Ben?"

He looks taken aback by my question, but he recovers quickly. "To see you. To talk to you."

"Yeah, well, you know we could have avoided this mishap if you would have communicated with me instead of ghosting me for two fucking weeks." I cross my arms. While I planned to sit next to him, to talk it out like adults, I'm too pissed now and need to keep my distance.

"I'm so sorry, Kelly. I know I fucked up. I want to explain. I don't expect you to forgive me, but I hope you can give me another chance to prove I'm not the asshole I've been acting like for the past two weeks."

I shake my head. "I don't know, Ben. I guess, start talking and we'll see where that gets us. You owe me one hell of an explanation."

"I know I do, baby."

Ugh, the name. "Don't call me that," I grit out, digging the back of my teeth into each other. His eyes sink, confusion at my words, so I add, "Don't use sweet names at a time like this. It won't get you anywhere other than pissing me off even more."

He nods. "I'm sorry."

I roll my eyes, wondering how many more times I'll hear those two words tonight. "Go on, start explaining." I wave my hand in front of me impatiently.

"I was offered a job. In New York. There's a whole list of pros and cons for both taking the job and not taking it. While it's with a great company with potential to grow into what I'm looking for, it's not a job I really want, and it takes me further away from you. It overwhelmed me." His shoulders curl as he rubs his hand over his head. He huffs out a breath to clarify. "The decision, that is. I couldn't stop thinking about it. Every waking moment, I was thinking about it. Every time I told myself I didn't want to be any further away, I'd counter back with the thought that we were in such a new relationship, and I shouldn't be this invested in it."

The moment the words leave his mouth, a sharp stab of pain lances through my heart. If I weren't leaning against the wall, arms already against my chest, I would have physically stumbled. Ben misses the moment, as he's had a hard time keeping my eyes, so by the time he looks up at me, I've masked the pain.

"You and I did not have an easy start. And we'd only been a couple for a month or so before I applied for the job. I'm used to being on my own, Kelly, so the idea of having to think about someone else just didn't register for me."

"I'm not loving this explanation," I mutter. But he keeps going.

"I shut you out because it made things easier. It was wrong, I get that. I hated it. I missed you so fucking much." His eyes are pleading, but I don't know what he expects from me. It's not going to be forgiveness.

"You missed me, but shut me out. That makes sense," I snap.

"Kelly, I know. It's all so fucked up, and it's hard to explain. When I told you I needed space, it was wrong. I just needed to figure out what to do. I was treading water, and I wasn't making any headway. I was close to drowning."

"You should have talked to me. That's what I'm here for." I realize at the moment, my tone is no longer laced with anger, but with sadness. "You actively chose not to confide in me." I choke on the words.

"I know," he says softly.

"I knew something was wrong. But you wouldn't talk to me. We were two thousand miles apart, and you wouldn't talk to me, Ben. It broke my heart." That's when a tear breaks free. I angrily brush it off my cheek.

"Come here, Kel," he says, holding out a hand to me. I shake my head. I can't get close to him. He reads my stance well and doesn't move toward me. "Please don't cry."

"I'm mad, Ben. And I'm fucking sad. I fell for you so quickly. Hell, it's stupid how quick it was. I knew you'd break my heart. I'm just surprised it didn't take long."

Whipping away more stupid tears, I find his face again. His shoulders slump, arms hanging at his sides. His eyes are red-rimmed, his expression slack.

"I'm so, so sorry." His voice breaks.

"What makes this even harder is that all I want in this moment is for you to hug me and tell me it's going to be okay. But I know it would just be a lie."

He stands at this, and with four long strides, he's in front of me, wrapping me in a hug. Breathing him in, the warmth of him circling around me, I lose it, sobbing into his chest. He only pulls me closer. My arms snake around him, and I grip the back of his shirt as sobs rock through me. He kisses the top of my head, but he doesn't tell me to quiet, he lets me have this moment of weakness. When the crying stops and I'm able to take deep breaths, he walks backward toward the bed. We sit, still embraced.

I hiccup, pushing away from him and wiping my eyes. He replaces my fingers, using his thumbs to dry my cheeks.

"I don't want to break your heart anymore. I don't

want to make you cry or cause you any pain. Kelly, I'm so sorry," he murmurs.

I don't say anything, not trusting my heart for what words might come out.

"I should have done this from the start. I should have asked you what you wanted. Would we be able to continue on if I moved to New York? I even should have..." He doesn't finish the sentence, his nose scrunching.

"Should have what?" I whimper.

"Nothing. It would have been selfish." He's mad at himself. I can see it in his face.

"Tell me," I demand.

He searches my face before he speaks. "I should have asked if you'd move to New York. Not right away, but down the road."

I'm stunned. "You were going to ask?"

"It crossed my mind several times, but every time it did, I was too scared it was going to scare you off. Our relationship was so new, asking you to move for me felt like too much, too soon. No one in their right mind would agree to move across the country for someone they'd just met." His face turns pensive. "The thing is, it never felt new with you. It's always felt like we'd known each other for a long, long time."

"I know," I croak. We're both quiet for a while—his hands never leaving me while I try to calm myself from my emotional outburst. Occasionally, he wipes away a stray tear.

I decide to give him some honesty of my own. "When I visited you in Chicago, I was about ninety percent sure that if you asked, I'd move there just to be closer to you. Then you got that phone call and shut me out. I went home feeling like a fool for thinking you'd want me around all the time. That all I'd ever be is some part-time lover—a long-distance relationship to you."

"Baby," he mumbles, and this time, I don't have the strength to yell at him as he pulls me into him.

"I kept telling myself that you'd never leave your beaches and sun for a city that saw its fair share of snow and cold."

"Well, you should have asked," is all I mutter.

"I should have done a lot of things. Here," he says. He stands up and walks into the bathroom, then comes back with a wad of toilet paper that he hands to me. "You're still leaking."

I see a ghost of a smile play at his lips, and I can't help it—I snort. Taking the tissues from him, I scoot further onto the bed.

"Thanks. I didn't mean to lose it. But stress mixed with a lack of sleep is a recipe for disaster."

He stays on the edge of the bed, careful to give me space, but not as much as before. I sop up my tears and blow my nose, not even caring how unladylike it is. But if I don't, I'll just keep sniffing up the remnants of my cryfest. He watches me while I do this. I ball up the toilet paper as I think about how I need to invest in a box of tissues.

"So. Where does this leave us, Kelly?" His hand lands on my knee.

I look at him and see that he's not expecting good news. Unfortunately, I knew before I even stepped foot back in this apartment that there wouldn't be good news tonight.

"I can't do the long-distance thing," I tell him softly.

He swallows. "I know. Me neither."

"You live in Chicago. Your new job is in New York." He opens his mouth, most likely to correct me on the fact that he hasn't accepted the New York job yet, but I shake my head. "If your career takes you to New York or keeps you in Chicago, we can't do this. There may be a chance down the road that I could move but, I'll be honest, I love it here. And I can't get to that point if I'm in a long-distance relationship."

"You see no future for us, then." His words almost break me, and with the way he nearly chokes on them, I know they're breaking him, too.

All I can do is shake my head. He scoots in, his hand staying on my knee as his other snakes behind my neck. Leaning in, he presses his forehead to mine. My eyes flutter shut as I take in this moment.

"Fate set us up to fail," he growls.

"Fate's a bitch," I reply.

"I'm sorry I wasted so much time, baby." His broken voice cuts me deep.

"I'm sorry too, Ben." He squeezes my neck. We sit there, head to head, eyes closed as we breathe each other in.

Then the tears start to fall again—slow, big, and more from a deep-rooted sadness than before. I wrap my arms around him and bury my head into his neck.

"Hey, no more of that," he whispers. He hooks a finger under my chin, lifting me away from his shoulder. He looks down at me. "Can I kiss you one last time?"

I slam my eyes shut as I force away more tears, but I nod. His lips are warm as they touch mine. He brushes his lips over mine again, and then on the third pass, I give my heart one last chance to say goodbye. I pull him closer and kiss him back with every emotion I've got left in me.

He groans as his tongue slides between my lips, and they part, letting him in. We kiss like fools. Like there's no tomorrow. I fight back a moan of sadness when I remember that for us, there isn't. This is it. Our last time together.

He leans me back on the bed, stretching out over me. And I let him. I let him take what he wants, because I know it's the last time I'll be able to give it to him. My heart won't be able to handle this in the morning.

We lay there on my bed, kissing, feeling, and doing our best to commit to memory every tiny detail about each other. Ben's fingers dance along my body, tracing every dip, every curve. He goes on kissing me as if our lives depend on it. Because right now, they do.

I BREATHE IN DEEP, doing my best to engrave his scent into my soul. For something to hold on to, anything, to cling to in his wake. My eyes lock with his, and like a slideshow, I recall every moment we've shared. I run my fingers over his face, trying like hell to remember the smile and frown lines. The curve of his nose and the grit of his five o'clock shadow under my hands.

Hours pass between us until we've somehow managed to make it under the covers, both still fully clothed. Want, *need*, boils between us but there's also a silent understanding that taking this any further, making love for one final time, will destroy us both.

The last words spoken between us revolve around me asking him when he'll be leaving. "I'll leave in the morning. I'll be gone before you wake," he murmurs hoarsely, his voice heavy and thick with sorrow.

"Hmm," I reply. The weight of it all, the sheer emotional exhaustion, is creeping in. It pulls me under like the current of the ocean until I can't fight it anymore. My eyes drift closed as Ben kisses my temple and pulls me in closer to him. His arms wrap around me while my head rests on his shoulder.

I can't pinpoint the moment the room shifts, but at some point comes the whispered plea, "I love you," before the distant sound of a door closing. I don't know if it was all a dream—a door closing on something special, a metaphor for where my life is right now—or if it was Ben leaving early enough to avoid a tearful goodbye.

All I know is that when I wake, I'm alone in my bed, the pillow cold beside me. The clock on my nightstand reads ten in the morning, and Ben is most definitely gone. It all feels like a dream, where any minute I may wake up and find that he's come back. That things are different and we're still together. Instead, it's a nightmare. A tragedy where both characters are left with a broken heart.

EIGHTEEN

Ben

I never saw myself as a coward, but that's what I fucking was this morning. I knew I wouldn't be able to leave her if she were to look into my eyes. Tears brimming over her long lashes while she said goodbye would have broken my heart into a thousand little shards. I did this to her. I couldn't blame her for not giving me another chance—I ruined us. I got in my head, shut her out, and tossed our future into the garbage.

So I took the cowardly way out. I left before she woke. Kissed her cheek, told her I loved her, and forced myself out of her bed. Sitting at the airport for nearly five hours was worth not having to say goodbye.

I didn't bother changing this morning. My black tee smelled like her. Holding her all night, after hours of kissing, it was all the goodbye I could handle. Sitting in the airport, I drowned in the memories of our time together and did a fan-fucking-tastic job of keeping my emotions intact.

With such a crazy week, the fuckery that was yesterday, and a painful breakup—well, I was in a shit mood.

I arrived home a couple of hours ago, took a shower, and am now sprawled out on the couch when there's a knock at the door. I groan because I really don't want to deal with anyone right now. But the knock comes again, and I push myself up and open the door. There are only so many people it could be, so I don't bother looking through the peephole.

Swinging the door open, I find it's the one person I really don't want to see, but I smile at her anyway. I motion for Bernie to come in, and I can tell as she takes me in that's she's reading my mood.

"You're back," she says as she passes me.

"Yup," I grunt and push the door closed with more force than expected.

"You're unhappy." She bites her lip before perching on the arm of the recliner.

"You're perceptive today," I mutter, throwing myself back onto the couch. "Look, I'm exhausted. I want to chill out today. I'm not really in the mood to talk."

I flip through the channels, hoping she'll go away. I'm being an asshole, I know.

"I take it things with Kelly didn't go well?"

I snort.

"Want to talk about it?" Her tone is soft.

"Still not in the mood to talk, Bern."

"I spent some time with Kelly before she flew home. We talked a bit about what's been going on, and she was pretty upset with you. Do you think maybe she just needs some time to work through it?"

"No."

"Are you even gonna fight for her?" she asks. I actually look at her for the first time, and her eyes are wide with concern and sadness.

"Why do you care?" I ask.

She looks like I just slapped her as she jerks back. "I care because you're my friend, and I really like Kelly."

I grit my teeth. "She ended things and made it perfectly clear we're through. There's no fight left in either of us. So get over it." She gasps, but I continue on. "It's for the best. Time to move on," I grumble.

It's not actually for the best—not for me—but there isn't anything I can do at this point. Kelly doesn't deserve a weepy asshole trying to talk her into taking him back.

The shake of her head gets my attention. A nasty laugh falls from her mouth. "I swear, you boys are shit at relationships. The whole lot of you. You screw things up and then get all broody and shitty when you can't sweet-talk your way out of things," she says to herself, but I'm offended.

"Excuse me?" I growl as she stands. *Good, she's leaving.*

"I love ya, Ben. But you're an idiot. Maybe if you'd start being honest with the people in your life, you wouldn't be so grouchy."

"What do you mean? I'm honest."

Sometimes.

"Right. Just do me a favor and figure out your shit. And do it soon. You lost a wonderful woman because you got lost in your head."

"I know," I bellow, shooting up into a sitting position.

My outburst doesn't faze her; she just keeps going. "Don't let it also cause you to lose friends and a career."

I blink.

"Tell us the truth about moving on and get on with it already," she spits. Then she stomps out the door and slams it behind her.

Fucking shit sticks. What just happened?

I got my ass chewed, that's what. I spend the rest of the day pissed—at Bernie, at Gallant Gaming, at my team, at myself. But never at Kelly. Mostly myself.

That night, when I take a cold as fuck shower, I decide Bernie was right. At least, maybe I can get this right. So I call a meeting for the next morning.

I make it a point to get to the training room early. I'm sitting in one of the leather chairs when the team starts to arrive. Bernie hardly looks at me, Simon and Dex don't act off at all, and Chuck doesn't say a word. Not that he ever does.

"What's up, Buttercup?" Simon laughs as he plops down at the end of the couch.

"I've got some stuff to talk to you guys about," I tell him, then look at each of my teammates.

"All right," Dex says cautiously.

"I'm taking a job with Gallant Games after the season ends. It's a permanent gig, so this is it for me." I swallow. Four pairs of eyes look back at me, not making a sound. I add, "I'm done. Gone. You'll need to fill my spot."

"Yeah, we got that," Dex says slowly.

"Then why aren't you saying anything?" I hesitate, thinking this was a bad idea.

"We're just surprised you told us. We figured we'd be finding out the day you packed up and flew out." Simon says.

"Seriously?" I mutter.

"You're shit at being open about things, dude." This comes from Chuck, and I slice my eyes to him. He's my roommate and honestly, he's never said anything like that to me before.

"What he said." Simon points to Chuck as he drags his eyes back to his phone. Chuck doesn't hold eye contact long, so I look at Simon and Dex. They don't look mad. I cut my gaze to Bernie, and her arms are crossed as she stares at her feet.

"I'm sorry for not telling you guys sooner," I say.

"It's not like we didn't figure it out pretty fucking fast, man. Gallant flew you out. You were asking about what our plans were after gaming. We're all pretty smart folks, Ben." Simon is normally the broody one of the team, but I guess since he fell back in love with his childhood sweetheart, that role has switched to me.

I look to Bern again; she hasn't spoken yet.

Dex speaks then. "It would be great if you could help us find your replacement."

I nod. "Yeah, totally."

"Bern, you got anything you want to say?" Simon asks her. Apparently, it hasn't gone unnoticed with the others that she hasn't said anything yet.

When she lifts her eyes, there are tears, but she doesn't let them fall. Blinking several times, she says with a shaky breath, "I'm happy for you, Ben. And I want the best for all of you guys. I know this can't last forever."

Dex reaches over and puts a comforting hand on her shoulder.

"Wow, Ben, consider yourself loved," Simon says with a chuckle. "She wasn't this broken up when Link left the team."

I smirk. He's not wrong. Link left a couple of years ago, Chuck was his replacement.

Bernie glares at him. "I wasn't broken up about it because I knew he wasn't going anywhere. Where Dex goes, Link goes. But Ben is *leaving*, leaving. And things are changing. Don't deny it."

Dex doesn't ease his grip, and Simon hangs his head. We all know it's true. I was just the first one to do something about it. I guess it's my way of protecting myself. Seems like I have a habit of hurting others before they can hurt me. *How's that working out for you, Benny Boy?*

We sit in quiet for a few moments before the door to

the training room swings open. In comes Link, oblivious to what just went down. He gets halfway into the room before he notices us all sitting there staring at him.

"Whoa. Who died?" he mutters.

"No one. Ben is leaving the team," Dex says coolly.

Link looks to me and with a grin, says, "Congrats, man. Gallant swoon you enough?"

Shit. Did they all know?

The question must show on my face because he chuckles. "We all knew it was coming. Plus, I talked to Ronnie at E3. They're excited for you to join the team." His face turns pensive. "Though, I never saw you for a community manager."

I bite back a groan. "Yeah, me neither. But that's what they're offering for now."

He studies me for a minute, leaning against the wall where it opens into the kitchen. "You know, there's no reason to rush into anything. If you're tired of these ugly mugs, except for that beauty in the chair," he jerks his head toward Bernie, "you can still step away. Take time to find the right job."

He isn't wrong.

I lean back in my seat. "I know, but I need a change." *I'm crawling out of my skin, and I can't risk these guys leaving me behind. I don't want to be the last man standing.*

He nods in understanding.

I don't expect Chuck to speak, but like normal, it's a shock. "I guess I'm just surprised you aren't moving out to get with that hot surfer girl. Am I right?" He grins and looks around the room. He's met with blank stares and most definitely a glare from the beauty in the chair.

"Shit," Simon mutters under his breath.

Gritting my teeth—fuck, my dentist is gonna get on my ass about the grinding—I manage, "Surfer girl has a name.

And we didn't work out." I'd like to tell him to show some damn respect, but I don't.

Bernie jumps out of the chair at that moment. "All right, meeting over. Let's get some gaming in. Then we can call Rob and let him know about Ben's plans."

And just like that, a weight is lifted from my shoulders. Or it should be. Yet there's so much left lingering in the air.

REGRET.

Never in my life have I felt regret—until now. For four weeks, regret has been hanging over my head like a storm cloud. A cloud I can't seem to get away from.

A month ago, my life started spiraling into a new chapter. Plans were set into motion. I left my heart in Hermosa Beach with a woman I would probably never see or hear from again. But it was better that way. And I was so caught up in the final month of our tournament season—finding my replacement and preparing for a new career—that the time I spent thinking about that woman was limited to my nights alone in my bed.

Fuck, I miss Kelly.

I loved Kelly early in our relationship—hell, maybe even from the moment I met her. I just wouldn't let myself believe it until it was too late. Look where that got me.

If there's one thing I've learned about myself over the last few months, it's that I'm shit at relationships of any kind. I have no one to blame but myself for what happened between us. And I should probably do a better job of fixing myself before I even think about getting involved with anyone else.

I'm also going to miss this team. I spent the better half of the last year figuring out a way to move forward. To not be left behind. I'm not the kind of guy that gets left behind. I do my own thing—what's best for me.

But it wasn't until the ink was barely dry on the signature belonging to my replacement when it hit me that I was done. And it hit me so damn hard. Guess that's what I get for trying to run away before I had a chance to be forgotten. I somehow managed to get hurt anyway.

Matt's his name, and he slid into the role like he was meant to be there. He's friendly and happy, about five years younger than me, wet behind the ears, and hell-bent on making his team debut into the pro gaming scene a splash.

His experience as a gamer is laden with excellent marks on tournaments he played in as a single. He specializes in a few games but has a love for *Call of Battle*.

Team NoMad is the perfect fit for him.

My replacement.

I didn't think I'd feel like this. Like a piece of me, another fucking piece of me, is being torn away. It turns out I was leaving those important pieces of myself strung all over the continent. Cali, Chicago. I'm not sure what it says about me running off to New York, the next chapter in my life incomplete. But it's what's going to happen. In five days.

My bags are packed. My room is nearly boxed up. I haven't sent any of my shit to New York yet. Call it procrastination if you will, but I'm not quite ready for all that. It makes it all... final. But it's packed, so at least there's that.

Matt will be moving into my room once I'm all out. Most likely within hours of me handing my key off to Chuck. But I still have five days before that's happening. This is still my apartment for five more days, and I'm going to soak in every last moment—every last memory of this place—before I have to say goodbye.

Gallant has set up an apartment rental for me. Apparently, they own a few near headquarters. I'm going to stay there for a couple of months until I can find something permanent. The relocation bonus they gave me will help, and I'm not hurting for money, so I know I'll find something nice.

That's about the only thing I'm looking forward to about New York. My own place. A *new* place. How fucking sad is that? That this job I decided to take—that ultimately ended my relationship and career as a pro gamer—isn't even the job I want?

I grunt as I shove the last of my books into a box.

I won't dwell on this anymore. It's happening and I'll deal with it. Maybe the job won't be as bad as I'm worrying it will be, and I'll learn to love it.

Right.

I don't have anything to really do over the next five days. Tomorrow, I'm spending the day with my parents. And Bernie mentioned a going away dinner. On instinct, I head toward the door to walk over to the training room, but as I approach, I remember I'm done. My gaming equipment is already set aside, ready for me to pack up. All the stuff in my room is my personal belongings. Most of the equipment items in the training room belongs to the team, but some were gifted to me by sponsors. I'm taking that shit with me.

I stop in the middle of the living room, staring at the door and deciding against collecting that stuff right now. I know the team is all gathered there, and I don't want to deal with Matt's excitement and the team's sad eyes. So I walk to the couch and flip on the television.

Mindlessly, I flip to *The Mandalorian* and hit play. But

my mind wonders before too long. Maybe I should stop avoiding the inevitable and move up my flight. Am I really going to just sit around for the next several days doing this shit? Nothing?

My phone dings from my pocket—an email. But I ignore it. A second later, it rings. With a sigh, I pull it out and look at the screen, swiping to answer.

"Hey, Gar," I mumble into the phone. I grab the remote and pause the show, realizing I'm going to have to start it over because I have no idea what's going on.

"Yo, Ben. Lasso just sent you an email." I can tell by his voice the dude is hyped up.

"All right. How much coffee have you had today? You sound…"

"Excited? Well, brother, that's because I am," he rushes. "What's the status on the Gallant job?"

I scratch my cheek. "Uh, I accepted it. I leave at the end of the week. Shit's all packed." I thought for sure he knew all this.

"You sign a contract with them yet?" He sucks in a breath.

"I have the contract, but it's not signed. Why?" I draw out the word. Why does he care about my contract?

"Fuck. That's good news." His tone is relieved as he lets out a breath. "Look, I know the timing of this is crazy, but Lasso wants you."

"What do you mean, they want me? I'm really not looking for more freelance voice-over gigs, Gar." I run my hand over my head.

"No, they have an Associate Producer opening. They want you."

My eyes narrow. "Associate Producer?"

"Yeah, the guy who had the job just up and left. His wife was relocated or something, and he put in his notice yesterday. Management has been scrambling because there's a new project starting up and they need this position filled. They're giving you the associate title to start, but the guy who left was at the executive level. You just have to show them how kick-ass you are, and you'll see a title change and pay raise before you know it."

"Tell me about the position," I say, dumbfounded. *Is this real?*

"Yeah, sure. It's right up your alley, Ben. You'll run the show from start to finish on a video game project. This is huge."

Shit, it's exactly what I wanted. "This almost seems too good to be true." I wish I could see his face to see if he's fucking with me right now.

"I know, but I mentioned your name in our management meeting this morning. They know you and like you, and when I told them about your new job with Gallant, they didn't want to waste a minute. HR already emailed you the full job description and an offer letter. I was standing in Darla's office when she hit send, but I wanted to talk to you before you read the email." His excitement is rolling through the phone and seeping deep into my bones.

"No interview? An offer just like that?" Again, too good to be true.

"Like I said, you've worked for them the past six months and they like you. They feel confident in what you can offer. I forwarded them your resume, and since I was already on your reference list, I gave you a fucking stellar reference." He laughs, and I have no doubt he did just that.

"Thanks, man. Holy fuck." I lean forward, elbows on my knees.

"Say yes, man."

"I want to, but Gallant is expecting me." I sigh. I hate

going back on my word, and while I may not have signed a contract yet, I don't want to burn a bridge.

"Yeah, I know. But this job is a perfect fit. You know damn well you have no desire to be a fucking community manager. You hate social media and that's what you're signing up to do for forty hours a week."

He's so damn right, but I'm not telling him that. I groan.

"You know what else this means?" His voice is low.

"Huh?" I grunt.

"It puts you thirty fucking minutes from your girl. No more long distance, man." I can hear the smile in his voice, and I hang my head.

No way Kelly takes me back. But the thought of being so damn close to her makes my chest ache where my heart used to be. Adrenaline courses through my body like a jolt of electricity—a shot of fucking caffeine straight to my soul.

"Don't mess this up again, Ben. If this isn't fucking fate helping you out one last time, then I don't know my ass from my face." He's right and I know it. I've never in my life believed in fate. I've got too much more important shit to think about than fate, and *what's meant to be will be* shit. But the night I met Kelly, then seeing her at the beach weeks later, I started to question it. I gave it a good long thought, and it's been a pain in my side ever since.

"Fucking fate," I murmur.

"Awesome fucking fate, man," he parrots.

"If I jump on this job, I lose my chance at Gallant. My spot on NoMad has already been filled."

"All you have to do is accept the job and it's yours. Benefits rival what Gallant offers. Salary is probably more than any community manager would make. And even if it's not, I know money isn't a deal-breaker for you." He's, again, not wrong. I hate it when he's right because he lets it go to his head.

"Shiiit." I sigh. "I want this job. I want California." I'm not naïve enough to voice that I want my girl back—that's something I might not get—but living close to her is a hell of a lot more manageable than living nearly three thousand miles away.

"Yeah, boi!" he yells.

Laughing at his excitement, I say, "You just fist-pumped, didn't you?"

"You bet your fine ass I did." He chuckles and I shake my head.

"What now?" I ask him.

"I'm heading back into Darla's office. Reply to that email accepting the job, and she'll help you from there." He mutters something to Darla and we say goodbye.

I review the email, offer, and description quickly, and I can't believe I'm looking at my dream job. I fire off a reply to Darla, and within the hour, I'm in a conference call with management and HR. My schedule to leave Chicago in five days works for them, but since I have to adjust my flight, I move it up by two days.

Suddenly, the need to leave Chicago behind is a need I can't fulfill fast enough. When I see Dex, Simon, and Bernie the next day to collect my equipment from the game room, I fill them in on the change of plans. Bernie cries. I don't know why she's so emotional. She's normally so badass. She has to be if she's going to be at the fucking top in this industry. But she hugs me, and while I already miss this group that's become family over the past several years, I know they aren't going anywhere. My time with this pro gaming team is now my past, but my future—well, she's in California, and I can't get to her fast enough.

NINETEEN

Kelly

One of the reasons I love the ocean is because when I'm out in the water, my mind isn't in overdrive. It's just me, the waves, the salty air, and the sun. It's a Tuesday morning, nearly Halloween. This portion of the beach is my favorite spot, I come out here early enough that I don't have to fight for space with other surfers. On the weekends, it's crowded. On the weekdays, not so much.

Straddling my board, I face the horizon as I let the water rock me into a natural rhythm. It's so damn peaceful out here. I would stay out here forever if I could.

A small wave rolls in, but I let it go. My mind isn't completely settled yet. I need to be one with the water before I chase the next one that rolls in.

I'm not due at the shelter until nine, and it's hardly even six in the morning. I could stay out here another two hours if I wanted. I may just do that.

I didn't sleep worth a damn last night—or the night before. My dreams the past two nights were filled with the man who got away. I was in Culver City visiting my cousin over the weekend, and I swear I saw Ben. I knew it was a mind trick, but it affected me just the same.

It was mid-morning, and I was on my way to Melting Moon Café and a man came out of the cafe that looked just like him. I saw his profile for a split second before he turned in the opposite direction. He was looking down at his phone, so I didn't get a good view of him. I stopped dead in my tracks and was jostled from my stare when someone bumped into me from behind. It was my fault—you don't just stop in the middle of a crowded sidewalk. My eyes dragged down his backside, looking for tattooed artwork across the back of his neck and down his arms, but the man was wearing a hoodie so my efforts were denied.

I closed my eyes and centered myself. It wasn't Ben. He's in New York living his life. I'm in California living mine.

But the idea of seeing Ben walking out of the café really stuck with me. The rest of the weekend, my mind wandered. I thought about what would happen, what I would say, if I ran into Ben again.

Would we hug? Would we smile at each other and catch up? Or would it be a quick hello and move on? What if he was with his new girlfriend? Not that he has one. I honestly don't know. But there's bound to be a time where that man finds himself a girl that's worth him settling down for.

What if when we meet again, I'm with my new boyfriend? Again, there's no new boyfriend, but it's only a matter of time according to my cousin and Aubrey. Both are champing at the bit to set me up. While I've told Darcy that under no circumstances is she allowed to set me up with anyone ever again, I may allow Aubrey to. As my best friend, I know she won't do me wrong. If I were out with a boyfriend and Ben and I saw each other again, would his eyes heat with jealousy? Would I want them to? Or would I want him to smile and wish me luck and be happy for me?

I let out a heavy breath as I idly run my fingers through the water near the side of my board. Maybe, given more time, I'll only want the best for him. For us to smile kindly at each other and move on. But right now, the thought of loving another, and him finding love with a woman that isn't me—well, I'm not ready for it. The feelings are big and they consume me if I'm not careful. I miss him.

I met him in March, and by August, we were over. Six months of missed connections, texts, short visits, phone calls, and sex. Amazing freaking sex. They were the best and most stressful six months of my life.

I splash my hand through the water, sending droplets flying.

"I've moved on," I say to the ocean.

The past several weeks have been wonderful. Okay, they've been meh. But the good news is that I still love my job at the shelter. And I can officially call it my job because the lady I was filling in for resigned two weeks ago. She decided she wanted to stay home with her newborn, and Aubrey offered me the job. She said she expected it would happen and knew that if she got me in there, I wouldn't want to leave. She was right, of course.

No, the past several weeks may have been rough, but the past six months were huge for me. Game-changing. I changed careers, found a job I absolutely love, moved into my own place, started surfing every day, fell in love, and then had my heart broken. That's a lot of shit jam-packed into six months.

Honestly, I wouldn't change it. Well, of course, the heart breaking part I would change. Who would want to keep that? But I fell in love with a good man, and my time with him was wonderful. I just wish I didn't miss him so much now. The last two weeks of our relationship may have sucked, but he'd become my best friend, and I fell for him hard and fast. In the blink of an eye, he was gone.

I shake my head. I need to get out of my mind this morning. Hell, if I looked up into the sky long enough, I'm pretty sure I would see his face in the clouds. That's how pitiful I'm being right now.

I take a big breath of ocean air and center my focus. I can see a wave rolling in, so I paddle toward it. It's time to enjoy the morning the only way I know how—with the waves.

I look down at my waterproof watch and see it's been more than an hour. I should head back to the beach. I take my time. There are more people on the beach now, the boardwalk opening up for the day. This is normal, which is why I like to get out here so early.

The hairs on the back of my neck rise as I see a lone figure standing on the beach. I can't see him well, but he's facing me as if he's watching me. I can't make out his features until I get closer. He isn't very close to the water, only halfway down the beach or so. As my toes connect with the ocean floor, I tuck my board under my arm and slowly continue out of the water. I study him—he's lean, tall, and dark. He has olive skin and dark hair, and he wears a black sweatshirt and board shorts. His hands are in his pockets. He holds nothing, and there's nothing beside him. He just stands there in the sand, alone. And I know without a doubt, his gaze is zeroed in on me.

It isn't lost on me that I'm not scared in the moment. I should be; I've clearly caught the attention of a stranger. But I'm not worried. I'm not scared because my mind is a nasty devil and Ben's name runs through it on a loop.

"No," I breathe. I have to stop doing this to myself.

The man takes a step closer. One step, two. Then a

third as the water hits my thighs. I grip my board as I realize the man slowly approaching me is, in fact, Ben.

My heart crashes against my chest like a head-on collision. My head spins, the water splashing against me as I stumble back a step. But I center myself and keep walking. There's no more water, just soft, wet sand under my feet. He's moving toward me now, with no hesitation.

My breathing is labored, and I try to gain control as we stop in front of each other, feet apart. I turn my board and lean it into the sand, using it to help me remain vertical.

"Kelly." His voice is exactly as I remember it. And it packs a punch right down in my lower belly. His smile, his face. Taking him in—a man I haven't seen in six weeks but have only dreamed about—causes my ovaries to twist with need. *Fucking hell, get yourself together, woman.*

"Ben." My voice is breathy and shaky. His eyes are wide, focused on me. His lips tip up on one side. I slowly reach my hand out and press my shaking fingers against his right shoulder. Feeling him beneath my fingers, I know he's real. Without taking his eyes off me, he reaches up and closes his hand over mine. My eyes drop to where our hands touch, his warmth wrapping around me like a bubble.

"Are you worried I'm not real?" His low, deep voice jerks my gaze back to his.

"Yeah, I guess so," I murmur.

"I'm very much real, Kel." My nickname is easy on his lips.

"What are you doing here?" I search his face.

"On this beach or in California?" He chuckles and a flurry of flutters fills my tummy.

"Both." Dropping my hand from his body, I lean into my board again. His being here makes me dizzy. I just spent more than an hour out in the water. Now, with my feet back on dry land, I still feel like I'm feeling the motion of the ocean.

"Let's sit. I don't want you to eat sand." He leans forward and takes my board from me, placing it gently next to me as I plop down in the sand. He steps to the other side of me, sinking to the ground. He kicks off his sandals and stretches his long legs out in front of him. I cross my legs, feeling the sand as it clings to my wet body.

I feel his eyes on me as I slowly turn my face toward him. "Why aren't you in New York?"

He takes a breath before speaking. "I didn't take the job."

I suck in a breath, my eyebrows raising in surprise. "What?"

He nods, pulling his gaze away and looking out at the water. "The job at Gallant wasn't what I wanted. I was settling. I was trading too many perfect things for a job I didn't want in a city I didn't want to be in."

"Where did you want to be?" My voice is shaky as I stare at his profile. His head slowly turns toward me, a sad grin on his face.

"Where you are."

My breath hitches as he looks back at the ocean.

"What happened?" I ask, just above a whisper.

"I had my room packed up and ready to move when good ole Garland called me and told me Lasso wanted to offer me a job. A full-time job that was right up my alley. So I took it."

I stop breathing. Literally, I have to force myself to take a breath.

"You took the Lasso job." I don't ask. I say it more to myself, joining him in his stare out over the ocean.

"I did."

We sit next to each other in quiet peace for a few

minutes. Our shoulders brush, but we don't touch. We don't speak. I don't ask the one question I want to because I'm scared of his answer. He shifts next to me, his hand finding mine in the sand between us.

I feel his stare, and I turn to him and look into his eyes.

"I've been living in Culver City for three weeks now. I didn't have an apartment set up when I got here, so I lived out of my hotel for the first week. I stored all my stuff in Garland's apartment until I found a place. I jumped right into my job, as I only got a week with the guy I was replacing. It's been three long fucking weeks." His laugh is low and unapologetic.

I nod. "I'm happy you didn't settle. I know what it's like to settle. Hating your job sucks." I swallow. "So that answers why you're in California. I'd still like to know why you're here right now."

His head tilts, a cocky smirk shining through his sadness. "I enjoy watching a certain surfer girl master the waves. I could watch her for hours."

I lean into him and bump into his shoulder. "Creeper." I hold back a laugh, but I'm unable to contain the smile on my face.

He dips his head, chuckling. "You're the most beautiful woman I've ever seen, Kel. No matter what you wear, or if you're hungover, or even right as you wake up. But when you're out there," he nods to the ocean, "you're fucking sexy as hell. You're mesmerizing."

My cheeks heat as I pull my eyes away from him, unable to let him see how his compliment is affecting me. I feel his fingers under my chin as he pulls my face so I'm facing him. "I'm here on this beach because I couldn't stay away a minute longer."

Looking into his eyes, I see desire and relief mixed with just a little bit of worry. I say his name, my voice trembling.

"I'm not asking you to give me another chance. Do I want one? Hell yes, I do. But I'm not expecting one. I just wanted to see you again. I wanted to tell you in person that I'm here and I'm not going anywhere." I close my eyes at his words. He leans into me, our foreheads touching.

I take deep breaths, trying to calm my roaring heart. It's not working, and I can't stop the single tear that breaks free.

A pained groan emits from his throat. "Baby, please don't cry."

"I'm not."

I feel his thumb swipe away the rogue tear as he chuckles softly. "My bad. Must be ocean water then."

I nod, not lifting my head away from his.

"Kelly?" My name is just above a whisper.

"Hmm?" My eyes flutter open, finding his own eyes shut.

"I'd really like to kiss you." He opens his eyes then, catching my gaze as he smirks. Which makes me smile.

"Then do it," I challenge.

So he does. His lips cover mine like a force to be reckoned with. He doesn't waste time on gentle, soft, tentative kisses. His kiss is demanding as his tongue plunges into mine. I let him take it all because I want to give as good as I get. His answering moan has me wrapping my arms around his neck and pulling him into me.

His hands are everywhere at once. One wraps around the back of my neck, then tangles through my hair. The other roams to my collarbone, then down to my breast. My back arches as he moves his hand back up to my neck, tilting my head so he can claim more of me. A distant whistle breaks through the blood pounding in my ears, and I slowly break our kiss. Our arms still embrace each other, and we both pant as we try to bring fresh sea air into our lungs.

On a ragged breath, I tell him the truth. "I missed you."

"So damn much, Kel," he adds. "Can I see you again? When you're ready, of course. I'll wait, I'll take your lead. Just, please, tell me we can try again. I promised myself I wasn't going to beg you, but after that kiss, I can't just let you go without fighting."

"This is you fighting?" I mumble.

"Get used to it. I'll fight for you every damn day for the rest of our lives. I won't give you up again, because I love you, Kelly."

I suck in a breath at his confession. "Promise?"

"Always." He kisses the tip of my nose.

"I love you, Ben." I lean in, kissing the side of his mouth as his lips grow into a smile.

He whispers, "Say it again."

"I knew I was in a world of hurt that first night we spent together. I fell in love with you hard and fast. You're this bad boy, sexy, sweet, and kind man. I love how you don't look like a nerd, but are one through and through." I kiss the other side of his mouth before adding, "The best part of my day has always been when you've been a part of it." Even over the roar of the ocean, and the voices and sounds behind us from the boardwalk, I still hear his breath hitch.

"You giving me another chance, Kel?" he asks in a shaky voice.

"No, I'm giving us another chance." I smile, then kiss his mouth. When I pull away, he's smiling and I'm smiling. We sit there, smiling at each other like loons.

The beach is getting busy, and I realize it's getting late. "Shit. I'm going to be late for work." I move away from

Ben as we both straighten. I push myself up and realize I'm covered in sand. My quick shower won't be so quick now.

"I've gotta get back to the city as well. When can I see you again?" His eyes are searching mine.

"Can you show me your apartment? Tomorrow evening?" I ask, running through my calendar and remembering I have dinner plans with Aubrey and Chance tonight. I would cancel, as I have dinner with them once a week, but I'll need to talk to Aubrey about Ben being back in my life. She isn't his biggest fan at the moment.

He nods his head with gusto. "Absolutely."

It's as if he didn't expect me to agree to see him so soon, but I giggle at his response.

"Come on, walk me to my car." Tucking my board under my arm, I hold out my other hand to him. He wastes no time threading his fingers with mine as we walk toward the parking lot.

Just like that, a weight of dread and melancholy has been lifted off my shoulders. It's as if all is right in the world now. My heart is full, and I can't wait to see what the future brings.

Epilogue

BEN

Nine months later...

"SHIT, THAT BOX WAS HEAVY." I wipe the sweat off my forehead as I stretch my back.

"What's in it?" Garland leans over as he walks into the room and places a box on the floor next to it.

"Fuck if I know. Kel, what's in this box? It's like two hundred pounds," I yell over my shoulder. Kelly is standing in the middle of our brand-new kitchen, the sound of tape ripping off a box coming from the same room.

"Just a sec," she calls back moments before she appears next to us. She leans over, looking for something, then nudges it with her foot.

"Oh, that's all my smut and sex toys." She looks up at me with an innocent grin as her eyes dart to Garland. I follow her gaze and see that his cheeks are pink as he stares down at the box.

Clearing his throat, he croaks, "Ah, well, cool. Very good." His head is bobbing up and down.

I grin at his expression before punching him in the shoulder. "Stop picturing my girl with a dildo in her hands, you bastard." Kelly laughs next to me, and Garland's head whips toward me and then Kelly. He glares at us both and mutters something about us being assholes as he walks away.

"Remember the free beer and pizza, man. Beer and pizza," I tell his retreating back. He flips me the bird as he walks out of the apartment.

I turn and pull Kelly into my arms as she's still giggling beside me.

"You're evil, baby." I smile, looking down at her.

"You're no better." She grins. I lean down and kiss her, something I've gotten to do nearly every day for the past nine months. Starting today, I'll be able to kiss her multiple times, whenever I want, every single fucking day.

Because, today, we move into our own place together. About fucking time.

We found a little bungalow not far from where Kelly was living over Aubrey and Chance's garage, and we closed on it yesterday. Today, we started moving in.

With help from our friends, we should have everything from my apartment in Culver City, and Kel's place moved in before lunch. With Garland, Chance, and I bringing in box after box and taking care of all the heavy lifting, we're tired. Kelly brings in what she can, but she's started unpacking and putting together the kitchen. Aubrey doesn't help with any lifting—she's six months pregnant—but at the speed she and Kelly are working in the kitchen, they'll be ready to move into another room in no time. Maybe we'll have this house unpacked sooner than Kelly and I expected.

"What's really in the box?" I ask her before she moves from my embrace.

"Just books." She smiles, but I narrow my eyes. She rolls hers. "For real, books. I packed the toys in my purse to ensure they weren't injured in the move."

She lifts up on her toes and kisses the tip of my nose before giving me a saucy grin and walking back into the kitchen.

"Evil woman," I say, and her answering, "You love it," over her shoulder causes me to laugh and shake my head. I head back out the front door, which we've propped open, just as Chance walks through with a lamp and two tote bags.

"Nice place you have here, mate." He grins.

"Thanks." I slap his shoulder as he passes.

The past several months have been great, truly. After that morning on the beach, when I told Kelly I was in Cali to stay, our relationship didn't struggle to pick back up where we left off. We saw each other multiple times a week, the way normal couples who aren't long distance start. But unlike a brand spanking new couple, we were getting a second chance to do things right. It was easy fitting into each other's lives; nearly effortless. Scarily so. It was as if the universe were offering up some kind of massive fucking apology for the shit we went through to get where we needed to be. Which was in the same state, less than thirty miles from each other.

Kelly and I started talking about moving in with each other a couple of months ago. We spent very little time figuring out where we would end up. I already knew I would live wherever Kelly was, and I also knew Kelly wanted the waves. So Hermosa is where we'll be. My drive into Culver City is easy. With traffic, thirty minutes. But if I timed my commute right, I could miss traffic, making the drive in less than twenty. I knew this because I often spent the night in Hermosa. Leaving Kelly late at night after dinner and hot sex was nearly impossible. Every damn time. On mornings after I stayed the night, if Kelly surfed, I left early. If we decided to sleep in and have more fantastic sex, I dealt with traffic.

My job at Lasso was everything I wanted when I thought about what I would do after pro gaming. The company, as I already knew, is great. My co-workers share the same love of the creation of video games that I do, which makes going to work each day enjoyable. I worried when I first took the job that I was going to burn a bridge with Gallant Gaming. But after being completely honest with them, that an opportunity I wasn't expecting came up, I couldn't pass on it. They were surprisingly understanding. I think they knew deep down, I didn't want what they were offering.

As I reach my car, I hear my phone ping with a text message. Before picking up the final box shoved in the very back of my trunk, I take a look at my phone and see I've gotten a text from Bernie about the group visiting when they're out at E3 next week. It's been a while since I've seen the team I left behind in Chicago, but we chatted on the regular. Kelly's become good friends with Bernie and has been added to a group chat with the girlfriends and wives of my old team. Apparently, it's a hell of a lot easier to foster a long-distance friendship than it is a relationship. But I love that my woman is involved with the women I respect and have considered friends for so many years.

It will be nice to see my old friends, show them my new place, and catch up on everyone's life. Bernie said they didn't expect an unpacked house, but I know with Aubrey's help, it's Kelly's mission to have this house put together and looking like a lived-in home before those Chicagoans showed up.

Kelly took the week off from work using vacation days

her boss forced her to take. Thankfully, after about two months of being back in Kelly's life, Aubrey was Team Ben again. Which is what Kelly told me went down in the weeks before and after our breakup. Chance was Team Ben, and Aubrey was Team Kick Ben's Ass. With the help of both Kelly and Chance, I was able to get back into her good graces.

Several weeks into our relationship, I invited the ladies —and Chance—to tour Lasso. To see where I work and meet some co-workers. That helped Aubrey big time—seeing I was really here and I wasn't leaving. My commitment to being in Kelly's life is never going to waver.

I shove my phone into my back pocket and snag the final box. Balancing it on my hip, I slam the trunk shut. One of the first things I bought when I moved to Culver was a car. Dropping eighty bucks on an Uber one way to Hermosa wasn't an issue when I was just visiting, but in the hopes I was going to get the opportunity to make that drive regularly, I knew I'd need to invest in a vehicle. Living in Chicago all my life, I never had a car. Yes, I knew how to drive. But I didn't have a need for one. Having a car now, at nearly thirty, feels good. Owning a home feels good. Living with the love of my life feels fucking good. It's only a matter of time before I'm officially making her mine. I have plans. They've already been set in motion.

I walk through my front door, blinking to adjust to the loss of the bright sun. Chance is sprawled out on the couch, panting like an old man. He's not, but since he's six years older than me, it's a fun taunt. Aubrey is waddling through the room, handing him a beer as she leans over the couch and kisses his forehead. Garland is hooking up the television. Kelly comes from down the hall, her soft smile lighting up the room as she sees me. I take several strides toward her, depositing the box on top of a stack three high.

"Hey there, handsome." She grins and wraps her arm around my waist.

"Sexy lady." We face the living room, taking in the space—our space. "This is a nice place you've got here, baby."

She nudges my side. "We've got it. And it is."

I look down at her as she tilts her head up, the distance between us not far. "You happy, Kelly?"

"So very happy, Ben." She rests her head on my shoulder.

"Me too, baby. Me too." I kiss the top of her head. She emits a soft sigh, and the sound alone is music to my ears. Suddenly, I'm wondering when we can kick these wonderful people out and start christening our brand-new house.

I let out a low groan, my grip on her tightening automatically with my very dirty thoughts. She gives me a knowing smirk before saying, "We promised pizza and beer, Ben. Pizza and beer."

"Get that pizza ordered stat, Kel. I'll only last so long," I tell her before I lean down and kiss her.

The End.

The Cocky Hero Club

Want to keep up with all of the new releases in Vi Keeland and Penelope Ward's Cocky Hero Club world? Make sure you sign up for the official Cocky Hero Club newsletter for all the
latest on our upcoming books:
https://www.subscribepage.com/CockyHeroClub

Check out other books in the Cocky Hero Club series:
http://www.cockyheroclub.com

I'm so glad you did. You challenged me to make my story the best it could be and without you, I don't think it would have turned out as good as it did. So thank you for that.

Amy and Allie, you are both so important to me. Thank you for dropping everything to beta read Cocky Gamer when you could have been playing Among Us instead.

A big thanks to Yvette, you're honestly stuck with me from now on.

Oh, and to Garland Thorpe for lending me his name without even knowing me. When I heard your name for the first time, the first thing out of my mouth was, "that sounds like the perfect story book villain." But after thinking about this character, I was going to create based solely on your name, I realized Garland made a much better best friend and so he was transformed into one of my favorite supporting characters to date.

Lastly, to all my readers, THANK YOU. Without you, there would be no reason for me to write. Every story I write, I write for you to enjoy.

Acknowledgments

As always, I'd like to thank my husband and children. Without my husband's support, I'm not sure I would be able to wear all the different hats I do and still be able to find time to write novels. Also, Sophia, Tessa, and Jack, it means the world to me that you guys love that your mom is an author. Thank you Mom, for always being the one to read my books, even when it might make you blush during sex scenes. To the rest of my family and friends who always share my social media posts about my books.

I'm so excited to be part of the amazing Cocky Hero Club world. Thank you to the amazing Penelope Ward and Vi Keeland for created wonderful books and giving myself and so many authors the opportunity to work with you.

A huge, massive thanks to my girl, Aubree Valentine. Without you I don't know what I would do when it comes to this whole author thing. From plotting, to fixing, to helping me spice things up when needed, you and that mind of yours is so valuable. I appreciate you.

My editor, Amanda, you stepped in last minute and

Other Books by Lauren Helms

Gamer Boy Series

Level Me Up

(A Love at First Sight Romance)

One More Round

(A Second Chance Romance)

Game All Night

(A Friends to Lovers Romance)

425 Madison Novels

Boyfriend Maintenance

(A Fake Relationship Romance)

Flawless Foundations

(A Best Friend's Sibling Romance)

Unexpected Expectations

(A Rags to Riches Romance)

Standalone Novels

The Love Hack

(A Contemporary Fairytale Retelling Romance)

Find out more about Lauren's other books on her website:
www.authorlaurenhelms.com

About the Author

Lauren Helms is a romance author her nerdy and flirty contemporary words. Lauren has forever been an avid reader from the beginning. After starting a book review website, that catapulted her fully into the book world, she knew that something was missing. While working for a video game strategy guide publisher, she decided to mix what she knew best--video games and romance. She decided to take the plunge and write her first novel, *Level Me Up*. Several published novels later, Lauren formed PR company, Indie Pen PR, to help other authors promote their books.

Lauren lives in Indianapolis, Indiana sharing her love of books and video games with her own Gamer Boy husband and three little kid nerds who will hopefully grow up to share the love of things that united Lauren and her husband on their own happily ever after.

Join my Facebook group!
    Lauren's Romance Game Changers
    www.authorlaurenhelms.com